MW01602881

LAZARUS MITI

The Prodigal Husband

KWELA BOOKS

All characters in this book are fictitious
and any resemblance to people, either dead
or living, is a mere coincidence.

Scripture quotations from the Holy Bible,
New International Version, with permission
of the Bible Society of South Africa.

Copyright © 1999 Lazarus Musazitame Miti
c/o Kwela Books, 28 Wale Street, Cape Town 8001;
P.O. Box 6525, Roggebaai 8012

All rights reserved. No part of this book may be
reproduced or transmitted in any form or by
any means, electronic, electrostatic, magnetic tape
or mechanical, including photocopying, recording,
or by any information storage and retrieval system,
without written permission of the publisher.

Cover: Pieter Wenning (1873-1921) *Portrait*,
oil on board, 27 x 20,5 cm. The original painting
is part of the Sanlam Art Collection, housed
at the Sanlam Head Office in Bellville.
Reproduced by kind permission of Sanlam Ltd,
2 Strand Road, Bellville
Book designed by Jürgen Fomm
Set in 10.5 on 13 pt Palatino and printed and bound
by National Book Printers, Drukkery Street,
Goodwood, Western Cape, South Africa

First edition, first printing 1999
ISBN 0-7957-0085-7

To Stephen Gersom Ngoma –
a friend indeed

ONE

Musa tossed sleeplessly in bed. Thoughts drifted in and out of his head. But one thing in particular kept returning. He rose and went out of the house. He considered his new wages – ten pounds. That was enough money. Surely, he could afford a second wife. One befitting a very important farm foreman.

Of course, Tisa was fine as the mother of his seven children. But a foreman's wife needed to be a little more fresh. He needed a young wife – one who would be no different from misisi, the wife of his white baas, except for the colour of her skin. A real African man deserved more than one wife. It was a sign of manhood and a measure of wealth. His younger brother, Shuzi, back home in Northern Rhodesia had two wives. His own father had lived with three. Why should he have only Tisa?

He came back into the house. His wife was singing hymns, despite the late hour. Musa sat quietly on his bed and listened to her singing, not wanting to interrupt her. They both attended the Dutch Reformed Church which Baas V.V. had built for his farm labourers. The thought of that Church worried him. It did not permit polygamy . . .

Tisa stopped singing and put her hymn-book away. Musa cleared his throat to speak. His wife had to know what was bothering him. But how could he start?

'Are you through with your singing, Tisa?' he asked.

'Yes, baba.'

'I have something important to tell you. Our household has grown big and the work is too much for you. I have decided . . .'

'Oh no, baba,' Tisa interrupted. 'Don't worry about a servant. That is for the rich. I can manage on my own.'

'That's not what I have in mind, Tisa. A servant would not help you much. What you need is a companion. I have decided to bring you a co-wife.'

'Baba!' exclaimed Tisa. And dead silence followed.

'Baba,' she resumed after recovering from her momentary shock, 'have you thought of the Church?'

'Of course! They say it is a sin to have more than one wife. But you know why they say that? They don't know our customs. Me, I will take another wife.'

'Please, baba, think again.'

'I have thought carefully. I can assure you it will be good for both of us. At your age, you need a helping hand. After having given me seven children, you deserve a rest. When your co-wife is here, she will do most of the domestic work. That's what junior wives are for.'

'Do you know what the Church will do to you if you go ahead with your plan?' asked Tisa. 'They will excommunicate you.'

'Let them. I don't care. I don't want us to suffer because of the white man's Church.'

'We won't suffer, baba,' pleaded Tisa. 'I may be the mother of seven children but I am not too old to work.'

Musa was no longer listening. It was Tisa's turn to toss. Even if she were not a Christian, she would not allow another woman to share her husband with her. She recalled the early days of their marriage. Her husband then wore a tattered pair of shorts. On top, he occasionally donned an equally ageing vest the colour of which was no longer distinguishable. His feet were rough and cracked from walking barefoot. Those were days when they could only afford one meal a day. Their diet consisted of nsima with beans, except on Wednesdays when V.V. slaughtered an ageing cow for his labourers. Musa was then a mere herdboy. He was such a considerate young man. Why had he changed? She recalled how he used to assure her that he would love her and her alone for ever.

When her husband arrived at V.V.'s farm, her father, Lwando, was the foreman. It was he who recommended Musa for the herdboy's job. Musa had arrived on a lorry with other young men who had been recruited from Northern Rhodesia. It was the foreman's duty to interview the recruits to determine what job would suit them best. When he talked to Musa, Lwando recognised the accent which reminded him of his home district in Northern Rhodesia. That familiar accent prompted him to interview the young recruit somewhat informally.

'Now, my boy, you must be from Northern Rhodesia.'

'Yes, baba.'

'Where in Northern Rhodesia?'

'Fort Jameson.'

Lwando smiled. He was pleased to have someone on the farm who came from his home district. But Lwando did not immediately tell the young man that he too hailed from there lest he became too free. A foreman was meant to be revered by every labourer.

'Don't they keep a lot of cattle in Fort Jameson?'

'They do, baba.'

'Does your father have some?'

'I have no father, baba. He died long ago.'

'I'm sorry,' said Lwando. 'Does that mean you never had the opportunity to look after cattle?'

'I looked after my uncles' cattle for some time.'

'So you know how to look after cattle?'

'I do, baba.'

Lwando decided that his homeboy should start by doing what he knew best. He would make a good herdboy. Tisa recalled how Musa became a favourite of her father's. As the years went by, he became even closer to her and her family till he ended up proposing marriage. Her parents gladly consented. Musa was a well-behaved young man with a good future. Because of his hard work, he rose through the ranks, becoming a kapitao and finally taking over from her ageing father as foreman.

Tisa looked troubled. What was happening to him? The devil was tempting him. Why was he contemplating taking a second wife? If he did, what would she do? Would it be proper to divorce him or would she have to accept living with him and the young co-wife? Divorce would be a sin. It said so in the Bible.

She rose, picked up a cloth bag in which she kept her Bible, flipped through some pages and then closed it. Looking up at the ceiling, she thought of which verses were relevant. She opened her Bible again and turned to one Corinthians chapter seven, verses ten and eleven, which she read silently:

> To the married I give this command (not I, but
> the Lord): A wife must not separate from her husband.
> But if she does, she must remain unmarried
> or else be reconciled to her husband. And a husband
> must not divorce his wife.

She closed the Bible and considered the scripture. The Word of God forbade divorce. If she separated from her husband, she would have to remain single for the rest of her life. If she left her husband and remained unmarried, what would become of her seven children? According to custom, her husband would take them all.

He had paid her father forty pounds as malowolo. This gave him custody of the children in case of a divorce. That bothered her. She was not going to leave her children under the care of another woman. She would have to live with her husband and his young wife for her children's sake. But would she be happy in a polygamous family? She had to reconsider the matter.

What did the Bible say about polygamy? Despite having been a thorough reader of the holy Book since her childhood, she had not paid any attention to its guidelines with respect to polygamy for it never occurred to her that her husband would contemplate taking another wife. Although he had not been a believer prior to coming to V.V.'s farm, Musa had slowly been converted to Christianity even before their engagement. By the time of their marriage, he had become so devout a Christian that he insisted on getting married in Church. But now, all that was beginning to wither away.

It was necessary that she seek the Bible's guidance on the subject. She would also consult the pastor. Perhaps he could talk her husband out of the idea. He might listen to him. Of course, as foreman, he was the most important black man at the farm, but when it came to spiritual matters, nobody was above the pastor.

Tisa's thoughts went on and on until she lay down beside her husband and fell asleep.

TWO

V.V. trusted Musa. When he made him foreman, productivity improved. For reasons he did not understand, his foreman was feared by every labourer. He became aware of Musa's leadership qualities when he was one of the seven kapitaos. He was the most efficient. And Lwando, his then foreman, also recognised the young kapitao's abilities. Whenever he was indisposed, Lwando would ask him to act as foreman. This arrangement was often made without consulting V.V., but he had no objection for he believed that his foreman knew the labourers better than he did.

As the years went by, Lwando began to delegate the duties of foreman more and more often to his son-in-law. V.V. noted it and decided that Lwando had become too old for the job. He retired him and put Musa in his place.

The labourers feared Musa when he was a kapitao. Now that he was foreman, they dreaded him even more. Since he came to the farm as a young man, most labourers found him in place there. Thus, he was the most senior of them all. One of the things that enhanced his authority was that nobody knew his background.

It was rumoured that he had come to Southern Rhodesia from Northern Rhodesia via Nyasaland in the early 1930s. Upon leaving his motherland, he spent two years in Nyasaland where he consulted the most powerful witch-doctors at a place called Nchisi. There, he was given various types of muti to help him find a good job and to make girls love him. It was further said that those witch-doctors boiled him alive in a mixture of roots and herbs to protect him from witchcraft. Thus, many labourers believed, it was not surprising that he married the foreman's daughter and later took over from his father-in-law.

As foreman, every man at the farm was under him. This included people whose job description required some formal schooling although Musa himself never set foot in a classroom.

People who said 'Ja baas' to him included teachers, the pastor, the store-keeper, the seven kapitaos and all the labourers.

V.V. consulted Musa whenever he wanted to discipline or dismiss a worker. Once a month, the workers' wives assembled at the farm store where Musa handed out their rations. He gave each household a bag of mealie meal, some beans, salt and sugar. Bachelors received their rations after work. V.V. did not employ women. But at one time, the school engaged a girl as a teacher. Her name was Rhoda. Initially, she joined the bachelors' queue for the provisions. Later, Musa decided on a special day for her. Gradually, he became attracted to her.

He had always been content in his marriage with Tisa, the mother of his seven children. But Rhoda was different. She was several years younger. She reminded him of what Tisa looked like when he married her. Secondly, unlike Tisa who had never been to school, Rhoda had completed Standard Four. Thirdly, whilst Tisa was from Northern Rhodesia, Rhoda was a local Shona girl.

There were other qualities he admired in Rhoda. One of them was politeness. Although employed as a teacher, she agreed to perform other duties he assigned her. She did some simple mathematical calculations for him when the need arose. One of these was calculating the number of days in a month that any labourer had been absent from duty. V.V. paid his farm workers on a daily basis. The baas himself made the payments but Musa kept a record of the number of days each worker had not reported for duty. Before Rhoda's arrival, Musa did all the number work. But with her around, he merely kept a register showing ticks for attendance and crosses for absence. At the end of the month, he passed this register over to Rhoda to add up the ticks and crosses for him, after which he submitted the totals to V.V. Only then did Baas decide how much to pay each worker.

Wages for labourers were low and nobody could afford a cut. So, they did their best never to be absent. They also ensured they were in Musa's good books for if he were not happy with them, he might put in a bad word about them to Baas. They knew Baas would listen to whatever Musa told him. They believed all that was due to the boiling in herbs he had endured at Nchisi.

The labourers further feared Musa because many of them were recruited by him. He had travelled to Fort Jameson in Northern Rhodesia and Fort Manning in Nyasaland to recruit men. Labour supply was abundant and the few whom Musa recruited considered themselves fortunate.

Musa enjoyed his position of power, but he sometimes envied the young labourers. They were at liberty to acquire any girls they admired when they pleased and to get rid of them when they felt like doing so.

But he, being properly married to Tisa, could not bring Rhoda into his house just like that. Tisa would not let him. Besides, people would talk and lose all respect for him as his authoritative grip on them would be compromised. He did not want that to happen.

In spite of those fears, he wanted Rhoda to be his and nobody else's. A beautiful and educated girl like her was fit only for a foreman. Wasn't he the greatest at the farm after Baas V.V. and his family? He had to do something to get her for himself. The only way he would acquire Rhoda and still retain his respect was by marrying her. There would be only one stumbling block – Tisa's Church.

Why did the Church prohibit polygamy when some great biblical figures were polygamists? According to the Old Testament, Abraham was a polygamist. And so were Moses and David. If these men who were in direct contact with the Lord had more than one wife, why was the Church prohibiting simpler men of today from marrying as many women as they could afford?

He was going to marry Rhoda whether the Church agreed or not. He would tell the pastor of his intentions. If the pastor objected, Musa would ignore him. He would make his proposal to Rhoda irrespective of what Tisa thought. Only after talking to his wife and Rhoda would he approach the pastor. Before tackling the pastor, he would study the Bible to equip himself with adequate examples of respected polygamous religious leaders of the Old Testament.

Musa again lectured Tisa on the advantages for both of them of bringing a younger woman into the family. His continued efforts, however, did not impress Tisa. That puzzled him.

'You must be out of your mind,' he told her. 'Our customs allow polygamy. If people back home heard that you were objecting to this, they would suspect that you were losing your brains. I come from a family that is famous for looking after more than one wife perfectly well. My father had three wives whom he kept happy till he died. My father's father also looked after three contented wives up to his death. And right now, my younger brother Shuzi back home has two happy wives. Why do you want me to destroy this family record which we cherish so much?'

'Baba, my late father-in-law may be forgiven because he did not know the way. But you have no excuse for you have received the Word of God.'

'You talk of the Word of God,' retorted Musa. 'I have told you before that I took that into consideration. There is nowhere in the Bible where it says it is a sin to have more than one wife. Where is my Bible? I'll show you some verses.'

Tisa handed it to him and he fumbled through the pages till he found verses which he considered relevant. 'Listen to this,' he said and began to read from the Book of Genesis, chapter twenty-five, verses one and six:

> And Abraham took another wife whose name was
> Ketura . . . But while he was still living, he
> gave gifts to the sons of his concubines and
> sent them away from his son Isaac to the land
> of the east.

He closed the Bible and gave it back to his wife without saying another word.

'Is that all?' asked Tisa.

'Is that not clear enough? Abraham was a polygamist. That is from the Bible.'

'But that is from the Old Testament.'

'And is the Old Testament not part of the Bible any more?'

'It is, baba, but some of those laws followed by the Israelites were later changed by our Lord Jesus Christ when he was on this earth.'

'Were they?' asked Musa. 'Well then, give me one verse from the New Testament where it is said that polygamy is sin.'

Tisa searched desperately for guidance from the Bible. She muttered each word, slowly dragging her finger line after line. Like her husband, she was a slow reader. Neither of them had received any formal schooling. They had been taught how to read by the lay preacher at the farm church who doubled as the sole catechist.

'Have you found any verse?' Musa interrupted her.

'Yes, baba. It tells about our Lord's original plan for marriage. Please listen to this,' she begged him, and then proceeded to read from the Book of Genesis, chapter two, verse twenty-four:

> For this reason a man will leave his father
> and mother and be united to his wife, and
> they will become one flesh.

Tisa kept her right index finger on that page, closed the Bible and then, satisfied with her reading, she gazed at her husband. But Musa laughed scornfully.

'Baba, this is the Word of God,' Tisa pleaded.

'I know it is the Word of God.'

'Why do you laugh, then?'

'What you read says nothing against a man taking more than one wife. It only says that the Lord sanctified marriage.'

'No, baba. Don't misinterpret our Lord's Word. The Bible does not say that a man would be united with his *wives* but with his *wife.*'

'Tisa, you are putting your words into God's mouth. You are interpreting the Word to suit your own wishes,' said Musa.

'No, baba. It is you who is twisting our Lord's Word to suit your own intentions.'

'No, I am not.'

'Please, you are. Just admit it.'

'Why should I admit something I know is false?'

'Baba,' Tisa began after a short silence, 'I think the problem we are facing is that we are trying to handle this matter all on our own. We need to consult other people.'

'I know what's best for us. There is no need for me to go consulting as if I were a small boy. I am a man. You too are not a young girl any longer. A mother of seven children is supposed to be consulted and not to consult.'

'Please, baba, no man can live without advice from his fellow men. The Lord made us differently. To some He gave one type of gift and to others, another. What you know, another man might not know and what another man knows you might not. Our problem is to do with the interpretation of the Word of our Lord. Since we do not agree, we need to consult the pastor. He will guide us accordingly.'

Musa did not know whether to agree with his wife or not. What bothered him was that the man of God was likely to agree with Tisa. The Church had talked against polygamy and its membership accepted that ruling without scrutinising the scriptures. Although he had not read the whole Bible himself, he did not think there was any biblical justification against polygamy. If there were any such justification, how come their pastor never quoted any verses?

Had all that talk against polygamy not been made up by ordinary men? Men who were incapable of acquiring more than one wife and looking after them well; men who were too lazy to feed and clothe more than one woman; men who were unable to father even a single child from any woman? Who was the sinner of the two: a man who married two or more women, made them each other's companions and remained faithful to them all throughout his life, or one who took only one wife but kept several girlfriends unknown to his wife and to each other? He wondered why the Church did not concentrate on breaking that sort of promiscuity rather than fight men who wanted to have decent and permanent relationships with more than one wife.

Musa was not afraid of the pastor. He would go to him and

speak his mind but he would not take any advice that would bar him from taking Rhoda as his second wife. Rhoda was fit for a foreman like him. He was capable of satisfying her. He did not have the kind of education that she had received, but that did not matter to a girl. What mattered was the means to feed her and clothe her. And he had those means. Who else at V.V.'s farm received ten pounds per month? None. Not even Rhoda's head-teacher. Not even the pastor himself. Only he, foreman Musa, got that kind of money month after month. He would keep the young Rhoda and Tisa, the mother of his seven children, properly fed and clothed . . .

He looked at Tisa. She was silent, with her eyes closed. He wondered what was going on in her mind . . .

Tisa was praying for him: 'Please, Lord, pull my husband away from the deadly grip of Satan. I know that with Your holy hand in this matter, my husband can be saved. I ask all this, Heavenly Father, in the name of my Lord and personal Saviour, Jesus Christ. Amen!'

When she opened her eyes, her husband was no longer there.

THREE

Musa had not revealed to Tisa the identity of the would-be bride. That could wait. It was more important to get her to accept the idea first. That was how it was done back in Northern Rhodesia.

He knew the procedure well, but his current situation was atypical. To start with, his wife had already objected to the idea of his taking a second wife. His other problem was that he had neither relations nor friends to consult. His only brother, Shuzi, was too far away in Northern Rhodesia. It would not do to consult anybody at the farm, for the workers expected him to take decisions on his own. The only people he could consult were his baas and the pastor. But neither of these would do. Baas knew nothing about African traditions whereas the pastor would insist that polygamy was sin.

Only one person needed consulting – Rhoda herself. If she agreed, nothing and nobody would stop him from marrying her. But first, he had to think of how to approach her. He shuddered to think what might happen if she refused to marry him. If she refused and then kept her mouth shut, all might be fine. But if, upon rejecting him, she chose to spread the news, it would be embarrassing and damaging since the workers would begin to imagine that he was not invincible. He enjoyed being revered. He would, therefore, have to handle his marriage proposal to her with utmost care. He also had to think of an appropriate venue. After careful consideration, he decided that the best place would be the farm store when she came for her monthly rations.

Before Rhoda was due to arrive at the store again, Musa had his entire strategy mapped out. He was not going to waste any time. As soon as she entered his office, he would go straight to the point. He had rehearsed it all. Firstly, he would summon the most authoritative variant of his voice. Next, he would ensure that his countenance had a well-balanced mixture of authority and calm that would signal to her that whilst he had no intention of coercing her into accepting his proposal, he would not be amused to receive a 'no'. He wanted to sound and look both tough and lenient.

'Rhoda?' he would start.

'Baba!'

'I know you are here for your rations – but I was looking forward to your coming today because I have something important to tell you,' he would say and pause to allow her to react. At this stage, so he assured himself, Rhoda would sit up and start to take him seriously. He told himself that she would anxiously respond as follows:

'Oh, what is it you have for me, baba?'

She would say this in a desperate and eager manner, thus encouraging him to say it all faster than he had planned.

'I would like you to be my second wife.'

In response, Rhoda would smile and then look down and start to bite her fingernails. And that would spell victory. Whatever would follow after that would be a mere formality . . .

But what transpired when Rhoda appeared before him did not compare favourably with what he had rehearsed. She knocked at his office door and before he remembered to summon his vocal authority, he let her in using the most ordinary version of his voice. She appeared more beautiful than she had ever done before. That made him doubt whether she would accept a proposal from a man of his calibre. She was a lot younger and better educated than he. It dawned on him that she would converse with V.V. in English if an opportunity arose, whereas the only tongue in which he spoke to Baas was Fanakalo. No, he didn't think he stood much chance. But then, he had decided to take a second wife and he had already informed Tisa. He was not going to retract his decision. So, when Rhoda stood in front of him, he offered her a seat and went on the offensive.

'Rhoda, do you have a husband?'

'No.'

That response derailed him for a moment. He had expected her to enquire why he wanted to know whether she had a husband or not. That way, he would have asked her to marry him. But her short 'no' answer seemed to have closed the topic.

He had to put himself back on course. After all, he was not simply a man, but the foreman and she, merely one of his subordinates.

'And are you betrothed to any man?' Musa continued.

'No.'

'No, no – is that all you can say?' asked Musa.

'But what should I say?'

'Something. Tell me more about yourself.'

'There is nothing to say. Tell me something about yourself instead,' said Rhoda.

'There is nothing you don't know about me. But, yes, I have something to tell you – something that has been on my mind for quite some time. I would like to marry you,' Musa announced.

'Ha!' exclaimed Rhoda.

'What's the matter?'

'You are married,' said Rhoda.

'Does that matter?' Musa asked.

'Your misisi will kill me.'

'Don't worry about her. Just tell me if you are willing to be my second wife or not.'

She looked straight into his eyes without blinking. She did not stoop and she did not bite her fingernails. She simply pierced her eyes into his.

'Say something,' said Musa.

'Well, give me my rations. I have work to do at school.'

'You haven't answered my question. Will you marry me?'

'No!' said Rhoda.

'Not again. Can't you say something better?' Musa asked.

'That's the best I can say. Just give me my rations.'

That was the end of his first attempt. He did not know how to interpret that response. Did she really mean 'no' or was she behaving like those girls back in his home country who insisted on a man going down on his knees before they would say 'yes'?

Now Rhoda had created another problem. Besides a wife who did not want him to be a polygamist, he had a girl who did not want to be his second wife. Only after sorting out the two women would he tackle the pastor. But how long would that take? Perhaps he did not have to wait till he convinced Tisa. She could wait. After all, she was already his. His biggest priority was Rhoda. She had to accept his proposal.

Banda was a lay preacher at V.V.'s farm church but everyone called him Pastor. In addition, they accorded him the respect due to a properly ordained priest. That made him feel good. Musa had a lot of authority and people feared him, but there were many issues which were not taken to him. For example, marital problems were not taken to the foreman but to the pastor. During the first weekend of the month, Banda visited every household to collect tithes. He also sat with the family for a while to enquire about the health of the children. And if he had heard some gossip about the relationship between a man and the wife, he would find some way of probing that as well. What he said and how he said it after collecting the tithe often depended upon the status of the given family. And so did the time he spent at each household. For instance, when he called on the foreman's household, he would sit there relatively longer, whether the foreman himself was home or not. Banda would sit with the foreman's wife and discuss the Bible.

Tisa was a voracious consumer of the holy Word, and each time that Banda called, she would have questions to ask about the Bible. Sometimes, her husband would get bored and leave the two of them to continue on their own. Whenever he called on the foreman's household, therefore, Banda expected to discuss the Bible, and he brought his copy along. The holy Book was like his walking stick. He never left home without it. Of course, he did not always have the opportunity to open it. At some homes, the only pastoral duty he performed was to say a prayer. But he was certain that at the foreman's home, he would require it. Not that he expected to discuss any problems with Tisa. She was the happiest of all the housewives at the farm. But to his surprise, when he next visited her, he found Tisa in a sulky mood. Her face showed that something was amiss and she did not receive him as warmly as she had done on previous visits.

'Sister, is everything well with you today? You certainly don't look well,' Banda commented.

'Pastor,' began Tisa after a moment of silence, 'indeed, something is bothering me. I was intending to see you about it. Praise the Lord, you are here today.'

'What is the matter, sister?'

'My husband,' said Tisa.

'Has he taken to drinking?' Banda asked.

'No, Pastor, something much worse than that. He wants to take another wife.'

'What? Does he not know it is a sin?' Banda asked.

'We have been arguing about it for some time. He insists that there is nowhere in the Bible where it says that polygamy is a sin. Perhaps if you spoke to him, he might listen. He tells me that Abraham, Moses and David were all polygamous. If you talk to him, he might take your advice,' said Tisa.

'Didn't you show him the scriptures?'

'That was my problem. I couldn't find any verses,' she said.

The pastor turned to his Bible and began to search for relevant scriptures. Together, they read from one Timothy chapter three, verses two and twelve and from Titus chapter one, verse six.

'Praise the Lord for the three verses,' said Tisa. 'I will read them to my husband. But I still want you to speak to him and to pray for him. Satan has entered his heart.'

'Yes, I must talk to him. In the meantime, tell him that you would like to bring this matter to the Church. As children of God, do not carry heavy loads on your own. The Lord does not want his children to suffer. Always ask and you shall be given.'

And Banda prayed for Musa and his family.

Her husband was in a bad mood when he came home, but Tisa was determined to keep her cool. She was not going to do anything that he could use as an excuse for taking a second wife. She would remain respectful and obedient regardless of what he did.

Musa walked straight into the living-room and sat on his chair which was designed to serve as a chair or a bed. That day, he immediately turned it into a bed and, as soon as he lay on it, he closed his eyes. Tisa followed him into the living-room and, kneeling beside him, she greeted him.

'How was your work today, baba?'

'Fine.'

It was clear that he was not in a talkative mood. So, Tisa left him alone and went to prepare the evening meal. As she set about her work, she prayed for courage and patience. She had to find the right moment to read the scriptures to him.

After supper, he remained mute. She wondered what was going on in his mind. Whatever it was, she would not allow it to prevent her from drawing his attention to the Bible. She let him lie there for some time whilst she cleared the dishes.

When she finally joined him, he was wide awake. Before confronting him, she said a short silent prayer. Then she cleared her throat and said:

'Baba, may I read to you something from the Bible?'

'What is it about?'

'You remember the other day you asked me to give you some verses which tell us that polygamy is sin? I now have three verses on that. You see, Pastor Banda was here and . . .'

'What? You talked to the pastor about this?'

'Yes.'

'And what did he say?'

'He confirmed that it is sinful for any man to have more than one wife. Listen to this:'

And she began to read: 'Now the overseer must be above reproach, the husband of but one wife . . .'

'Tisa!'

'Baba.'

'Stop that noise. I want to sleep.'

'But, please, it's only three short verses.'

'I don't want to listen to your reading. The God I know did not say that a man must never have more than one wife. If Banda wants to have one wife, that is up to him. Me, I want to have two. Besides, if I want to read anything from the Bible, I will do so on my own. I know how to read.'

When he had said this, Musa began to snore. As he snored, he thought about Rhoda. How many times would he have to talk to her before she accepted his proposal? She was the main obstacle. Tisa was not a problem. She had told him that she did not want him to take another wife. And so what? Those were mere words. If Rhoda accepted, and he went ahead with the preparations for the marriage, there was nothing that Tisa could do. As for Banda, he had raised that sort of objection only because it was his job. Musa was not afraid of disagreeing with the pastor, but he was not going to confront him just yet. Instead, he would summon Rhoda to his office in the farm store the following day and once again persuade her to marry him . . .

'Tisa!'

'Baba!'

'Why don't you go to bed? You are dozing.'

'Thank you, baba,' she said.

As she lay in bed, she sulked at the thought that her husband was resisting listening to the Word of God. She made up her mind not to talk to him about that problem on her own again. The next time she discussed the matter with him, it would have to be in the presence of the pastor . . .

FOUR

He did not summon Rhoda to his office the next day, but when she next called for her rations, Musa had prepared a fine speech for her.

'Rhoda,' he said, 'I have asked you this before but I will ask you again because I mean every word that comes out of my mouth. I love you and would like you to be my second wife. I could have told you one or two good lies. For instance, I could have told you that I will divorce my wife and marry you. That is what many men tell young girls when they want to turn them into their concubines. I am not going to tell you any such lie. I am not a liar.

'If a man tells you he is going to divorce his wife in order to marry you, don't listen to him. That man could be lying. If he were not lying, it could be worse. If a man divorces his wife in order to marry you, don't accept his proposal. If you do, one day he will do to you what he did to his first wife. He will have no problem divorcing you in order to marry yet another girl. Me, I love you and I want you to be my second wife. When you become my second wife, I will look after both you and your co-wife well. You might have heard that co-wives spend their lives quarrelling. In some cases they go to such extremes as seeking muti in order to bewitch each other. You know what causes that?' he asked and paused.

Rhoda laughed.

'What makes you laugh?' he asked.

'I have heard stories about polygamous men being turned into imbeciles through muti administered by their wives.'

'Co-wives resort to such jealousies only when they are not well looked after. When they feel that their husband is biased in favour of one of them, each will do anything to win his attention. But if he looks after them well from the start, no such trouble befalls him.'

'And will your wife be happy to have a co-wife just because

you promise her that you will look after her as well as you did when she was your only wife?'

'I will not merely promise her. I will look after her – and you – very well. In fact, I should treat her even better when she is not my only wife than I ever did when she was alone.'

'Why?'

'Because when she was alone, if I mistreated her, she would not think I was doing so because I loved another woman better. She would assume that I was in a bad mood. That's all.'

Rhoda laughed again and Musa joined her a bit uncertainly.

'There you go laughing again,' said Musa. 'Did I say anything funny?'

'But you also laughed.'

'You caused me to laugh. I mean business but it seems you are taking it as a joke. Now, tell me, will you marry me?'

Musa tried to look into her eyes, but Rhoda avoided his gaze, looking down at the unpolished cement floor of the small cubicle that served as his office. Then, she cleared her throat and looked up at him.

'Please, baba, I can't answer your question today. Give me time to think it over.'

'Sure!' said Musa. 'Take your time. This is not a small matter. It is wise of you to want to think it over carefully. When will you tell me?'

'I don't know. When I am ready, I will let you know.'

Musa did not want to push her any further. He did not expect her to come back with a negative response.

But many days passed without hearing from her. It was only when her monthly rations were again due that she reported to him.

'Have you been well?' he asked.

'Yes.'

'Why haven't you told me your response to my proposal?'

'Oh! Are you still interested in marrying me?'

'Of course,' said Musa.

'I thought you had changed your mind because for the whole month you did not ask me about it,' she said.

'Rhoda, don't treat me like a child. You know why I did not send for you. Hadn't you asked me at our last meeting to give you time to think over the matter? I have not changed my mind and I will never do. Now, tell me, will you marry me?'

'Please give me my rations,' she said.

Musa laughed. And Rhoda joined him instinctively.

'Please, my rations,' pleaded Rhoda.

'Do you want me to tell you the truth?' Musa asked.

'Yes, please.'

'I will not give you your rations until you tell me whether you accept my proposal or not.'

Rhoda looked up into the ceiling for a while. 'You know what I think?' she began. 'I think you are a determined man. Why don't you give up?'

'Do you want me to give up?'

'No!'

'Then tell me your decision.'

'I think you should approach my parents,' she said.

'And yourself? What do you say?'

'If my parents accept, I won't object.'

Musa sighed with relief.

'Good!' he said. 'You may have your rations. If all goes well, this might be the last time that you are here for them.'

Now that Rhoda had accepted his proposal, he would confront Banda, Musa decided. There was no point any longer in hiding the truth from him.

And then he would get back to Tisa. Now that Rhoda had agreed to marry him, his next duty to Tisa was to reveal to her the identity of her co-wife-to-be. And if Tisa continued to object, only the pastor would agree with her. And the pastor did not matter. Banda was not his relative. He wasn't Tisa's relative either. He was merely performing his duties. He was human and could make mistakes. He was not only human, but also an African man. Moreover, he was a Ngoni like him and Tisa, and was bound to agree that there was nothing wrong with polygamy.

That evening, Musa was in a jovial mood. Tisa wondered why, but she would not ask him lest he relapsed into irritability. She decided to take advantage of his hearty mood and re-introduce a discussion of the scriptures which Pastor Banda had given her.

After supper, Tisa dismissed her children to their respective huts as usual and then joined her husband in the main house where she found him studying the Bible.

'I am glad you are studying the Bible, baba,' she said. 'Can we read some verses together?'

'Which book do you want us to study?' Musa asked.

'Not a whole book, baba. I thought we could get back to the verses I wanted to read to you some time ago, the ones about the importance of a man having only one wife.'

'I was expecting that. Let us go ahead,' Musa agreed.

'Please turn to the following: one Timothy three, verse two; one Timothy three, verse twelve and Titus chapter one, verse six,' she dictated. When he was ready, she began to read from the first Book of Timothy, chapter three, verse two:

> Now the overseer must be above reproach, the
> husband of but one wife, temperate, self-controlled,
> respectable, hospitable, able to teach . . .

'Ye-e-s,' said Musa sleepily. 'And the next verse?'

'Verse twelve of the same book,' said Tisa, 'tells us that "A deacon must be the husband of but one wife and must manage his children and his household well." Our third reading is from the Book of Titus,' she continued:

An elder must be blameless, the husband of but one wife, a man whose children believe and are not open to the charge of being wild and disobedient.

'May the Lord bless His Word!' Tisa concluded and turned to her husband, only to catch him dozing. 'Baba, you are sleeping!'

'I am awake.'

'You heard the Word of our Lord on marriage?'

'Ye-e-s.'

'What have you to say about it?'

'Who? Me? Well, you know my position. I don't believe that our Creator ever commanded that every man should have one wife. You are misled by these pastors who don't understand the Bible. They twist it to suit their own human designs. I don't want us to quarrel over this, Tisa,' he said. 'We have been happily married for many years and I do not want us to make each other unhappy now. Together, we have seen our children grow. It would be unfortunate for us to start quarrelling at a time when our daughters are old enough to be married. It is also for that reason that I feel you, being the mother of seven children, deserve to be respected. You need to rest. That is why I decided to bring you a helper into this house.'

'But baba, I don't need any helper. I can do all the work alone the way I have always done.'

'Don't interrupt. I have something new to tell you. Do you know the girl I want to bring you as a co-wife? You will get on well with her. She is a polite girl. Her name is Rhoda, a teacher at the farm school.'

Tisa's reaction surprised him. She stood quietly, looking at him. Why was she so indifferent? He had expected her to tell him what she thought of Rhoda. Had she reacted so little because she had known all along who the girl was?

'What do you think about her?' he asked.

'Rhoda is indeed a good girl,' said Tisa.

'You approve of her, then. Can I approach her father?'

'No.'

'Why not?'

'The issue is not whether you have chosen the right girl or not. What we have been talking about is the morality of taking a second wife. I don't want you to marry another woman because that is against what the Bible teaches us. I have no grudge against Rhoda. What I am against is polygamy.'

'So, you won't change your mind?'

'Never!'

'I won't change mine either. Besides, Rhoda has accepted my proposal and I am not going to let her down,' he said.

'I think we ought to take this matter to the pastor,' said Tisa.

'I know what the pastor will say. Is he not the one who has been teaching you all these things? If it will make you feel better, we can see him. I was intending to inform him myself. As it is also your wish, we may go together,' said Musa.

FIVE

Rhoda came from a large family. Her mother was the second of her father's seven wives. Musa had enquired from her about her family background before dispatching a team of emissaries to her people. It had been a pleasant surprise for him to learn that Rhoda's father was a polygamist. He later learnt that Rhoda's entire family were Christians whose sect permitted polygamy.

This revelation raised Musa's hopes. He did not expect any opposition from Rhoda's people. Since her father had seven wives, he would not bar any of his daughters from getting married to a man who only had one other wife.

So, Musa's marriage to his second wife was smoothly arranged and Musa was satisfied with himself. The only assignment left for him was the impending confrontation with Pastor Banda. He would rush it now that Rhoda's people had given their consent.

But the foreman's imminent marriage to Rhoda had become common knowledge, and because the news was spreading rapidly, Banda decided that it was high time that he spoke to the foreman. He was not going to wait for Musa to take the initiative. Banda took his wife along with him and, after the greetings, announced the purpose of their visit.

'Baba, my wife and I wish to apologise for paying you such a surprise visit,' he began. 'We are here to discuss your marriage. We have heard that you intend to take another wife. We have also heard that the girl you want to marry is the young teacher at the school. We know that your mama is against you going into such a marriage. And we agree with her. What we have come here now for is to share with you what the Bible says about marriage.' The pastor paused and. Musa cleared his throat.

'Pastor, I am glad you came. I was intending to see you. Excuse me while I get children to prepare a lamp for us.'

Banda was the first to speak when the four of them were all seated, their Bibles at the ready.

'Before we continue, my wife and I would like to hear directly from you if it is true that you intend to take another wife,' said Banda.

'I do,' said Musa. 'In fact, arrangements for the wedding are now in place. I only have to pay the bride price.'

'But you are a Christian, baba. It is wrong for a child of God to have more than one wife. These are not my words but the Lord's. Let us turn to Deuteronomy seventeen. I will read from verse sixteen: "The king, moreover, must not acquire great numbers of horses for himself . . ." Now, let's move on to verse seventeen: "He must not take many wives, or his heart will be led astray. He must not accumulate large amounts of silver and gold."

His audience remained silent and the pastor continued. 'My wife will now read some verses from the New Testament.'

'Our first New Testament reading is taken from one Timothy three, verse two, which goes as follows: "Now the overseer must be above reproach, the husband of but one wife, temperate, self-controlled, respectable, hospitable, able to teach . . ."'

'Thank you, mama,' the pastor cut his wife short. 'Now go on to verse twelve.'

'"A deacon must be the husband of but one wife and must manage his children and his household well."'

Musa remained calm as the readings proceeded. He was not bothered by all that the Bible said. After all, those New Testament scriptures were not being read to him for the first time. His wife had read them to him before and he had reflected on them . . .

'Our final reading comes from Titus chapter one, verse six,' continued Banda. '"An elder must be blameless, the husband of but one wife, a man whose children believe and are not open to the charge of being wild and disobedient." Here end our readings for this evening,' Banda concluded. He kept quiet for a while. His wife coughed and Tisa moved restlessly on the reed mat which she shared with Banda's wife. The two men were sitting on stools. Other than those isolated sounds and movements, dead silence reigned.

Musa decided to make good use of the moments of silence. He geared himself up for a tough defence. He was going to tell the pastor that none of those verses affected him. All those verses referred to people of a particular standing in society or in the Church. He was going to tell the pastor and his wife and Tisa that according to those verses, only kings, overseers, deacons and elders were supposed to have one wife. He would remind them that he was not a king, nor an overseer, nor a deacon, nor an elder. But he would wait for his turn to speak. As soon as the pastor gave him the opportunity, he would go straight on to his defence. And the pastor would know that he was not foreman for nothing. He would make Banda aware that he was conversant even with matters pertaining to the Church and the Bible.

Banda's wife coughed again. She immediately followed that cough with a long yawn. Tisa also yawned pathetically.

Banda decided to break the silence. He cleared his throat and spoke solemnly: 'Let us bow our heads in prayer.'

And he prayed for Musa and his entire family. He asked the Lord to guide Musa and make him understand that what he was intending to do was evil. After they all said 'Amen!', Banda's wife yawned again and her husband closed the Bible study session for that evening.

'Brother Musa and sister Tisa,' he said, 'we will leave you now. But as we depart, we would like you to reflect seriously on the readings we had from God's holy Book. We also wish you to know that you have been in our prayers from the day we learnt of this problem. We will continue to pray for you. May the Lord be with you and your children.'

Musa was confused. Why had the pastor not given him the opportunity to argue his case? When he recovered from his state of confusion and disappointment, the pastor and his wife had left. Musa spoke to his wife.

'Is that what you call a Bible study?'

'What was wrong with it?' asked Tisa.

'We didn't discuss anything,' said Musa.

'Was there anything to discuss? The pastor played his part well. It is now up to us to play ours.'

'He did not play any part. He just wasted my time.'

'Please, baba, don't be so harsh with a man of God. Pastor Banda did what he had to do. You said all that was left was for you to pay the bride-price. What did you expect him to do after that? Did you expect him to promise you that he was going to raise the bride-price for you from church? He told you what was good for you to do and not what was good for you to hear. He told you that polygamy is a sin. He read to you proof from our Lord's Word, and ended the session with a prayer for us. Now it is up to you and I to reflect on God's Word. It is our marriage which is at stake and not the pastor's. If we choose to break it, we will have only ourselves to blame.'

'Have you finished your story?' Musa asked.

'Yes, baba.'

'Thank you. Now listen to mine. I am marrying Rhoda. I am doing this because it is good for you and for me. Soon, I will be bringing Rhoda here to be your helper.'

'Baba, I have told you before that I don't need any helper.'

'Don't interrupt me. Rhoda is the right kind of helper you need because she comes from a large polygamous family. Her mother is the second of her father's seven wives. Her mother and her six co-wives live in harmony. Now, in those Bible readings of yours, your pastor was unfair. He should have given me the opportunity to argue my case. I do not believe that the Bible forbids polygamy. The verses he read do not concern an ordinary man like me. Those verses are meant for kings, over-seers, deacons and elders. You know I am not a king. I am not an overseer. I am not a deacon. And I am not an elder.'

'Baba, you are an elder. If a man who has seven children and is a farm foreman is not an elder, then tell me who is.'

'You are putting your own words into God's mouth. The elder that the apostle Paul wrote to Titus about was an elder in the Church and not a leader of farm labourers like me,' Musa countered. 'I have also been studying the Bible. You must read the whole of chapter one of that Book to understand Paul's message to Titus. Do not choose a single verse just because you want to interpret it your own way.'

SIX

The thought of witnessing her husband's second wedding nauseated Tisa. She wished her mother were around to comfort her. But her parents had since returned to Northern Rhodesia. Her father had been retired in order to make way for her husband. In V.V.'s words, he had been relieved of his duties as foreman due to 'loss of vigour'. She had not minded her father being retired then as V.V.'s preference for her husband worked to her advantage. But now she felt her allegiance change from her husband back to her father. Perhaps if her husband had not become foreman, he would not have grown so big a head as to contemplate taking another wife. Her father was back in his village in Northern Rhodesia and her mother was his faithful companion in suffering.

Tisa would not contemplate divorce. That would be sin. She recalled the scripture in one Corinthians seven, verses ten and eleven: 'To the married I give this command (not I, but the Lord): A wife must not separate from her husband. But if she does, she must remain unmarried or else be reconciled to her husband. And a husband must not divorce his wife.'

Besides, if she divorced her husband, he would keep her children, and his young wife would ill-treat them. She would have to devise some means to discourage him from marrying Rhoda. What if she threatened him with divorce if he took another wife? She had nothing to lose by giving him such an ultimatum.

They rarely talked to each other those days. Communication consisted of commands from her husband and short responses or requests from her. Musa's daily repertoire would include such imperatives as: 'Give me water to drink; prepare a bath for me; make me some tea; polish my shoes,' and so on. Sometimes, he would only ask questions like: 'Where is my hat? What happened to my umbrella? Who broke my teacup?'

In turn, she only did as he commanded or responded in a

short phrase. She would say: 'Here's your tea, baba; your bath is ready, baba; I don't know, baba.' At times, she executed her orders without a word. She found that sort of life boring and unpleasant. She wished someone would put a complete halt to it. But who? Only her husband could bring back normality into their home. All he had to do was approach Rhoda and say: 'I can't marry you any more. My Church won't let me.' Or could she do it herself? Would it be as easy for her to confront Rhoda and say: 'Leave my husband alone, you devil!' Was she capable of such a violent confrontation? It would be humiliating. What if the young woman challenged her to a physical fight? That would embarrass not only herself but her children as well. Her only chance lay in her scheme to threaten her husband with divorce.

Tisa harboured this idea for some time, not knowing how to introduce it. But it did not take long before her husband prompted her. He had told her that he had paid the bride-price for Rhoda and that the wedding would take place any time.

'You are not getting married,' she responded in a flash.

'I thought this matter was now settled,' he said.

'No, it is not good for you to marry at your age. If the Church is immaterial to you, at least consider your children. Will they be happy to see you marry a girl of their age?'

'That is your own imagination. I am marrying Rhoda.'

'You still want to have two wives? I don't think so,' she told him. 'I am not going to be a co-wife. If you want to marry her, you must first divorce me.'

'I cannot do that, Tisa. The Bible forbids it,' he told her.

'If you do not divorce me, I will divorce you.'

'Tisa, that is against the Bible. If you divorce me, you will be committing a sin. And I know you do not want to do that. Secondly, do not forget that I paid malowolo for you. Before you divorce me, you will have to give your father good reasons. That I intend to take a second wife will not strike him as a genuine reason. Think about that.'

'I know I cannot divorce you without consulting my parents. But once I explain my reasons, they will understand. For that reason, I request that we go back to Northern Rhodesia to explain this matter. I will give my story and you, yours,' said Tisa.

'That is alright with me,' Musa responded. 'We will travel to Northern Rhodesia if that is what you want. But before we leave, the wedding must take place.'

'No!' Tisa protested. 'Why should you marry before you explain to my parents? We must first take the matter home. If you marry before we go, what purpose will our trip serve? If that is the case, you may as well divorce me first right here.'

'I am not going to divorce you. Even if I had to, I would not do so in the absence of your father.'

The journey from Salisbury to Lusaka took them three days by train, and that from Lusaka to Fort Jameson, two days. By the time they got to Katawa bus stop, they were all exhausted.

It was approaching seven in the evening when the family trekked homewards. Tisa led the procession and her children followed according to their ages. Musa walked behind everybody. Tisa carried a heavy suitcase in addition to a lantern in one hand and the baby on her back whilst each child carried their own bedding and clothing. Musa carried a walking stick in one hand and a torch in the other.

As they walked, Musa imagined how excited his brother Shuzi would be to see him. He thought about his cows. They must have multiplied. But what of witches? For the first time since they left Southern Rhodesia, he was beginning to regret that they had set out for the trip.

They branched into a narrow path off the main road which soon vanished. Tisa called out to her husband for help. Musa lit his torch and his eldest son Isaki spotted a cattle path. Musa now led the family and Tisa took his place at the rear of the procession. A few minutes later, they could hear the sound of drums. Then the smell of cow dung filled the air. Dogs barked and a man came out of his house. Outside, the man met Musa and his family. He squatted and greeted all the strangers, one after another.

'What has befallen us at this time of the night?' asked the villager after the greetings.

'Do not let your heart be tormented, baba,' Musa began. 'I have just arrived from Walale with my family and I want to be directed to the house of my brother Shuzi.'

'I am Shuzi!' the villager exclaimed. 'The spirits of our ancestors must have slept on my right-hand side. I understand the dreams I had last night. May the spirits of our fathers be praised!' The villager paused and called out to his two wives.

'Zenji! Nyanya! Your big husband is here,' he announced. 'At last, I too will be somebody. Our family will be big enough to build a village of our own,' he said. Walking towards the children, he struggled to study their faces in the dark.

'Who is this one? Children of Walale grow like pumpkins. Who is Maria?' he enquired about the only child of his brother's whose name he remembered. When his wives came out, it was their turn to marvel and then to shake hands with everyone. Even the baby on Tisa's back went through this hand-shaking ritual.

Shuzi led the family to his senior wife's house, carrying the suitcase which had fatigued Tisa. That suitcase was heavy. He wondered what it contained. Nyanya, Shuzi's senior wife, led all the children into the kitchen while Zenji, the junior of the two, began to prepare food. When she had attended to the new arrivals, Nyanya also set about preparing a meal for them. She instructed her sons to catch the fattest cock.

Whilst his wives were busy cooking, Shuzi walked to the headman's house to let him know of his brother's arrival. The headman informed his nduna. The nduna, who was the headman's assistant, went to the back of his house and got onto his ant-hill whereupon he began to address the entire village.

'Obaba! Omama!' he roared. 'Here's an important message from the headman. Firstly, Chief Nzamane has ordered all men and women of his land to go to his court tomorrow. He has hired a witch-doctor to catch witches. He wants us to know who has been eating our children. Nobody should remain.

'Now, here is the main item for this evening. We have been

blessed by our ancestors. Our kinsman, Baba Musandivute has arrived from Walale. Let us all go to Baba Shuzi's house to welcome him and his family. Thank you!'

Women marched to Shuzi's house with basketfuls of maize meal and dried pumpkin and bean leaves. Men went there too, knobkerries in their right hands. Zenji, Shuzi's junior wife, brought a dish of nsima with chicken. This was eaten by the sons Isaki, Yosefe and Luka. Nyanya, the senior wife, also brought nsima with chicken which was eaten by Tisa and her daughters. Musa did not eat with them. Shuzi and his two wives noticed this.

'Baba,' began Nyanya, 'is it the chicken you dislike or do you disapprove of the cooking of your village wives? You men of Walale want to eat food prepared by women who have been trained by wives of white men.'

'No, my sister,' protested Tisa. 'We women of Africa are always women of Africa whether we live in Walale or not.'

'Why, then, is our husband not eating our nsima?' asked Zenji. 'He must be hungry after the long journey!'

Tisa turned to her husband and gave him an accusing look. 'Defend yourself!' she told him.

'My dear wives,' Musa addressed his two sisters-in-law, 'forgive me for not eating your nsima. I don't eat nsima late in the night. It upsets my stomach. I take tea.'

'Listen to that,' Zenji told her co-wife. 'We should have known. We know that men from Walale cannot do without tea.'

'But where can we find tea at this time, baba?' Nyanya asked Musa. 'What can we give you in the absence of tea?'

In the silence that followed, the nduna whispered into his wife's ear: 'This muchona is proud. Leave him alone for now. He does not know what life is like here. Now he may refuse to eat nsima, but one day, he will eat sand.'

The headman's wife stole away to her house. She put a tablespoonful of sugar in a pot, placed the pot on the fire and fried the sugar till it turned dark. Then she poured water into the pot. The boiled water looked dark brown. This, she poured into a kettle and with it, she stole back to Shuzi's house where she handed the kettle and its contents to Nyanya.

'Who made me this tea?' Musa asked.

'The headman's wife,' Nyanya told him.

'Thank you, mama,' he said. Pushing two fingers into a small side pocket in his trousers, he drew out a two shilling coin. 'Here's some money,' he said. 'Thank you for the tea.'

The headman tugged at his wife's skirt and she understood.

'No, thank you, baba,' the headman's wife told Musa. 'It is kind of you, but as a guest, you are not supposed to give away any money because you will need it for many things.'

'Do not worry about that, mama. Yes, those are wise words but two shillings cannot build me a house.'

'Please accept the money,' said Tisa, taking over the persuasion from her husband. 'We are grateful to you all for welcoming us back home. We thank our Father in heaven for that. Unfortunately, we cannot thank everybody in the same way because we are poor.'

Although she was persuading the headman's wife to accept the money, Tisa was not pleased with her husband's action. She did not like the idea of handing out money to anybody for anything. That would arouse jealousy in the minds of the witches. She did not want anyone to think that her husband had brought a lot of money. That was why she made it clear that they were poor. But her word convinced the headman's wife and she accepted the money.

The money argument over, Musa went into his brother's house and brought out a paraffin tilley lamp which he lit. The brightness of its light perplexed the villagers.

'It is as bright as witches' fire,' said the nduna.

But Musa was not quite finished. After lighting up the lamp, he entered his brother's house again and walked out with a pot-shaped wireless set. The villagers crowded around it. Musa shook his head to the rhythm of the music coming from the set.

The nduna whispered into his wife's ear again. 'Look at him,' he said. 'See how he is shaking his hornless head like someone who is about to tear through a whole forest. This man is mad.'

Musa, however, did not continue shaking his head for, soon after that song was over, the valves of the wireless set burnt out.

Suddenly, there was no more sound from the thing. Shuzi stood up and shouted: 'Ah, these witches! On my brother's first day in the village, they have bewitched his wireless set. We shall see if they can eat that iron.'

Musa smiled. He knew his set could be fixed. For the moment, however, he took it back into the house and returned with a gramophone and began to play some records. The villagers were speechless at first. Then everybody started to sing along with Musa as the record which he had put on was a familiar one. In addition, it was in their language.

As people sang, Tisa and her children began to doze. And Nyanya, noticing that the guests were tired, showed Tisa and the children where they would be put up for the night.

The nduna was always up at dawn. As nduna, he was required to make announcements first thing in the morning and just before bedtime at night. He liked this aspect of his duties. If a month passed without an announcement, he felt bad. That morning, he was happy for he had something to announce. He climbed on his ant-hill where he reminded everyone to visit the guests from Walale. Thereafter, he told them once again of the need for every man and woman to go to Chief Nzamane's court that day where Kamchimba the witch-doctor was going to smell out the witches.

Many went to Shuzi's home to see the family from Walale. As they had done on the previous night, they took presents. By the end of the day, Musa had received mealie meal, chickens, eggs, beans and dried pumpkin leaves. The headman's wife took another potful of tea. On seeing the gifts, Musa stood up to address the people, but his brother whispered to him and they went into the house.

'Baba, last night, you gave two shillings to the headman's wife just because she gave you tea. This morning, people will give you more presents. Do not give them any money. That is not how we do things here. This land is full of witches. If you hand out your money like that, they will bewitch you and all your heirs so that they may inherit your property. These people are greedy. If you give them money, they will milk you down to the last penny and then laugh at you.'

Shuzi paused and looked his brother straight in the eyes. Musa responded with an expressionless face.

'Remember our in-laws,' said Shuzi. 'You have to give them something when they come to see you. If you give away everything now, what will you do when they are here?'

Musa stared at his brother and went out of the house. There, he thanked his kinsmen for the gifts and promised to find a way of expressing his appreciation in kind some day.

When Musa finished his short speech, the nduna rose and announced that it was time for them to leave for the chief's court where the witch-doctor was waiting.

That afternoon, the people of Nkhanza were back home. Kamchimba had declared their village witchcraft-free but nobody was pleased with his verdict. If it was true that their village did not have witches, where did their children disappear to every year?

They assembled once again at Shuzi's home two days after the arrival of his brother. He had invited them for a little celebration. Shuzi thanked them for having welcomed his brother. As their husband spoke, Nyanya and Zenji went into Nyanya's house and returned with two potfuls of a sweet drink prepared from mealie meal and millet. Men salivated as they expected to be served with beer. Shuzi knew he had to apologise for his inadequacy before the men set their eyes on the drink.

'Obaba, I am ashamed of myself for giving you these pots to drink. You deserve beer, but since my brother arrived only two days ago, all I can offer you is thobwa. My wives will brew beer for you soon. For today, may we all cool down our hearts with this water of the frogs,' Shuzi concluded and his wives began to serve the drink.

When everyone had tasted it, the nduna rose to speak. 'Obaba, I thank Baba Shuzi for giving us this thobwa. But I believe that it is his wives who have made it available to their fellow women and their children. We expect Shuzi to offer us men's drink. That he was not expecting any guest is not a good excuse. A real man ought to keep two or three bottles of kachasu,' he advised and paused. Shuzi smiled.

'I advise Shuzi to keep beer in his house if he is to remain a man like all other men. Our man from Walale must also learn to send a message in advance about his home-coming. If he continues coming to our village without warning us, he will find that the village has moved to a distant land.

'I trust that my brothers have learnt something. Now my wife will bring kachasu. That way, men can leave the thobwa to women and children,' the nduna concluded.

Men then drank and rejoiced. Musa, who did not drink beer, listened to his kinsmen. Many of them spoke. Later, they took to singing and finally began to dance to their own music. Then, an elderly man coughed and spoke from his seat.

'My children,' he began, 'I call you my children because I have finished more maize barns than anybody else in the whole village. I am grateful to our ancestors for having made it possible for me to be seated amongst you today and to talk to you when all those who looked after cattle with me are long gone.

'Musandivute, my child, your father and I looked after cattle together and fought many fights against each other and against people from neighbouring villages. I hear that you have four sons. That is good for Nkhanza because it is boys who build a village.

'A man who has boys must have cattle. One day, his boys will have to find themselves wives. For them to bring those wives into this village, they will need cattle. I therefore offer you a small cow which will produce enough cattle for you to build your own kraal in future. I hear that you share a kraal with your brother. That is all right but at one time or another, every real man must have his own kraal,' the elderly man concluded. Thereafter, the headman addressed the gathering.

'Obaba, omama, I thank you for coming to welcome your kinsman from Walale. Before we disperse, I wish to ask you for more co-operation. Baba Musandivute will soon need a house and I ask you all to assist him when he starts building. Secondly, I beg anyone who has any field lying fallow to lend or give it to our kinsman before the rains come. Lastly, let us all thank Baba Sakala for offering a cow to our kinsman.'

No sooner had the headman made that appeal than the nduna rose and proposed a vote of thanks in the customary manner.

'Yo Sakala!'

'Yo Sakala!' the entire gathering roared.

SEVEN

Tisa's parents, Lwando and Mwaziona, were seated outside their house when three messengers arrived. Neither of them recognised the boys. That worried them. Mwaziona knelt beside the boys and greeted them in a trembling voice. One of them reassured her: 'Mama, do not be alarmed. We bring you good news from Nkhanza. Your son-in-law and his wife and children arrived from Walale last week.'

Lwando breathed a sigh of relief whilst Mwaziona threw herself into the air with ecstasies of jubilation. 'My daughter! My grandchildren!' she shouted.

When she recovered, she had a fat cock slaughtered for the messengers and, as the boys ate, she placed ten live chickens in three baskets. After their meal, the messengers bade Lwando farewell.

'My children,' said Lwando, 'you brought us good news. Mwaziona and I are old. When our children are far away, we neither eat nor sleep well. We worry that something bad may befall them. We are glad that our son-in-law is back. Tell him that we will see them in a week's time.'

'And give seven of those chickens to my daughter. They are for my grandchildren,' said Mwaziona. 'The other three are yours.'

Women began arriving at Lwando's home one after another, anxious to know what had sent Mwaziona into all that jubilation. The news spread to every corner of the village: Musandivute, the muchona son-in-law of Baba Lwando was back!

Talk about Musa started doing the rounds. Some said that he had a car which he drove all by himself. Others said he did not eat nsima. It was also said that he did not speak Cingoni but Cilapalapa only. Musa had become a white man, a muzungu. Only his skin had remained African. All this was said by people who did not care whether anyone heard them or not. But when headman Mtendere rose to speak, everyone listened.

'Obaba, omama, I would like to ask Baba Lwando one question.' He paused, drew a miniature bottle of snuff from the pocket of his all-weather coat and sniffed out of it three times before turning to Lwando.

'Our son-in-law has given you both cimalo and malowolo. But have you given him his vipheko?' he asked. He was referring to the special beer brewed by parents-in-law for a deserving son-in-law, which was to be drunk at a special ceremony celebrating a good marriage.

'No,' said Lwando. 'Our son-in-law has not come home with his family since he married my daughter. Now that they are all here, we will soon prepare his vipheko.'

'Do so quickly,' said headman Mtendere. 'What will his people say if he begins to have grandchildren before he receives his vipheko? They will say there are no men in Mtendere.'

That Saturday, Mwaziona began brewing beer. And on the day that Lwando had promised to visit their son-in-law and his family, the beer was ready. Three elderly women and several young ones carried the beer to Nkhanza. They left Mtendere before dawn.

When the rooftops of Nkhanza came into sight, they stopped. With the pots on their heads, they stood motionless and began to sing and ululate loudly enough for the women of Nkhanza to know that some women were bringing vipheko. The women of Nkhanza organised themselves and rushed to welcome their guests. They could hear Musa's name featuring prominently in the visitors' songs. They were praising him and calling him a real Ngoni man.

That afternoon, the people of Nkhanza gathered at Shuzi's house to welcome the carriers of vipheko and to drink the beer and the thobwa. The drinking went on until many began to sing and dance. Musa played his favourite record on his gramophone. As the record played, he sang along and shook his head with nostalgia. It was a song about people who had migrated from Fort Jameson in Northern Rhodesia down to Lusaka or, in some cases, further south across the Zambezi to the tobacco farms in Southern Rhodesia. The more adventurous ones went further south across the Limpopo where they found employment in the mines of Johannesburg.

As he played this song, Musa thought of Rhoda, his wife-to-be, and wondered if she was still waiting for him. He wondered too what his father-in-law would say about his intention to take another wife. Of course, Lwando wouldn't stop him. Nobody would stop him. But somehow, he wished Tisa could take it more kindly.

It was at this moment that Lwando and Mwaziona arrived. When the nduna saw them, he shouted 'Yo Lwando!' The response that came from the drunken lot cheered Lwando and Mwaziona. As they entered Nkhanza village, Lwando proudly told himself that what he and his wife were experiencing was the dignity befitting a man and woman whose daughter was properly married. He couldn't help feeling that his son-in-law deserved two more vipheko.

They were all smiles as the nduna led them to his house. They had to be taken there because tradition did not permit them to enter their son-in-law's house. That included the house of their son-in-law's brother. Anybody who wanted to see them had to go to the nduna's house. Musa was no exception. He went there that same evening. He had to speak to his father-in-law. He was eager to get that difference between him and his wife over with. Rhoda might not be so patient as to wait indefinitely for him.

After the greetings, Musa kept silent, not knowing how to introduce the topic. The silence between the two in-laws continued until the nduna joined them. As soon as the nduna had taken his seat, two young women arrived with a whole potful of beer. With the arrival of the nduna and the beer, the atmosphere livened up. Lwando talked to his son-in-law freely. The more he drank, the freer he felt and the more he talked.

'Father of Isaki,' Lwando addressed his son-in-law, 'you and I should no longer fear each other. We must feel free to eat together and even drink together because you have given us seven grandchildren. Soon, your daughters will be married and that will make you a father-in-law as well.'

'Father of Isaki, those are words,' the nduna chipped in.

47

'Whenever you wish to tell me anything,' said Lwando, 'do not go through an intermediary. Say it directly to me. Do you understand me, father of Isaki?'

'I do, baba.'

'Now, tell me how you have been living with your wife out there at V.V.'s farm. Have you been alright?'

'I thank you, baba, for the vipheko. I am grateful to you and to my mother-in-law for honouring me. I also thank you for wanting to know how my wife and I have been. Baba, as you have said, Tisa and I are no longer young for we have grown-up children. That we have been able to raise our children to the age they have reached is a sign that we have lived happily. So, I have no complaint against my wife.'

The nduna shouted, 'Yo Lwando!'

'Tisa and I have been happy since you left us at V.V.,' Musa continued. 'However, recently, we began arguing. I say one thing and she says the other. Because we could not agree, I decided to bring the matter to you, baba.'

'What is this argument, father of Isaki?' asked Lwando.

'It is a small matter, baba, but Tisa makes it look like it is a huge problem. A few months ago, I thought of taking a second wife to assist Tisa in our home. But when I told her, she objected. That is the only problem I have with my wife, baba.'

'My son,' Lwando began, 'this is not a problem. Your wife has no right to object when you decide to take another wife. How many wives a man wants to have is his own decision. In fact, it is his right. A Ngoni man is free to marry as many wives as he can afford. So, do not listen to your wife. Now that you have told me, leave it to me. I will talk to mother of Isaki.'

'Hum!' the nduna exclaimed. 'Baba Lwando, have you ever seen things such as these? How can a woman tell her husband not to take another wife? Just what is this world coming to?'

'Those are the ways of the women of Walale, baba. There, some women behave as if they were men. That is why it is not right for any true Ngoni to marry women from Walale. A muchona who wants to be truly married must travel home and find himself a proper wife here.'

The nduna laughed.

'Thank you for those words of wisdom, baba. I knew you would understand,' Musa said. Then he bade his father-in-law and the nduna good night. He walked away a satisfied man.

As Musa left the nduna's house, his wife and children arrived. Tisa's mother, who had been with the vipheko women, also joined them. Tisa presented her children to their grandparents.

'My child,' began Mwaziona, 'we are proud of you. What you have done, giving us grandchildren, is the best thing a daughter can do. I am sure our son-in-law is equally happy with you.'

'Mama, those are words,' the nduna commented.

Drinking, singing and dancing continued at Shuzi's house. Lwando and Mwaziona heard the people of Nkhanza shower them with praises. This went on until they fell asleep. The following morning, the last vipheko pot was brought out and stood under a big tree where the beer would be drunk ceremoniously. Everyone attended the ceremony. They were all smiles as they entered the second day in the celebration intended to cement a successful marriage. Lwando and Mwaziona sat on a cowhide, in seclusion, at a distance from the tree where everything was taking place.

By midday, the celebration was nearing its climax. There was going to be a dancing competition. The women of Nkhanza formed one circle and those of Mtendere, another. And there, under a big tree, the competition began. The two teams danced the citelele dance. Each team did their best to outsing the other. This turned the singing into a mere mumble-jumble as there was more effort to produce the loudest noise than to utter the actual words of the songs. In the long run, the women of Mtendere sang so loudly that those of Nkhanza could hardly be heard. Feeling helpless, the women of Nkhanza gave up dancing and watched their victorious guests with admiration. Tisa, filled with joy and pride, joined her kinswomen. For a moment, she forgot her worries.

The three elderly women of Mtendere also joined their team. One of these waved their emblem in the centre of the circle. Then the women of Mtendere stopped singing and took to shouting and jumping about in a disorderly manner. The woman who carried the flag began to run from household to household and all the women of Mtendere ran after her. When they got to one household, they stood there and threatened to remain there for life if they were not tipped. Lastly, they came to Shuzi's house where they demanded to be tipped before they carried their empty pots away and set off for Mtendere. The defeated women of Nkhanza followed their victors happily and saw them off for quite a distance.

Lwando and Mwaziona stayed in Nkhanza two more days. Before their departure, Lwando sent for his son-in-law and his daughter so that he could speak to them in the presence of his wife.

'Baba and mama,' Lwando addressed his son-in-law and his daughter, 'we are happy to see you after a long time. We are particularly pleased to see our grandchildren. That you have seven children means that you have had a successful marriage. I commend you for that. I thank you, baba, father of Isaki, for looking after our daughter and our grandchildren so well. You are no longer a son-in-law. You are now our father. Mwaziona and I are ageing. We look to you, baba, to feed and clothe us. For that reason, we do not expect you to quarrel. If you do, who will look after us?' he asked and paused.

'Now, let me address myself specifically to mother of Isaki. I have been told by father of Isaki that he plans to take a second wife and you, mother of Isaki, do not want him to. Mother of Isaki, tell your mother and I here and now. Is it true that you do not want your husband to take another wife?'

'Yes, baba.'

'Where did you get such ideas from? Since when did women begin to control their husbands? Your husband is free to marry another woman in the same way that he was free to marry you.'

'Baba, I have always been polite to my husband and I want to continue to be. But I do not want him to take another wife because it is a sin. My husband is a Christian and knows that polygamy is a sin.'

'May I say something?' Musa began. 'Tisa is right that I am a

Christian. But I do not agree that polygamy is a sin. She knows that there is no verse in the Bible which forbids it.'

'Thank you, Baba father of Isaki, for those words. But I do not care what the Bible says about polygamy. What I want is for you two to continue to be happily married. You have children to look after. You also have us to care for. So, mother of Isaki, let your husband marry whomever he chooses. Once he has married, learn to live well with your co-wife. She will be your companion and helper. She is not meant to be your enemy.'

Then Lwando bade his son-in-law and his daughter farewell. But that was not the end of the issue for Mwaziona raised it again after the departure of Musa and Tisa.

'Baba,' she began, 'I did not want to talk in the presence of our son-in-law. I want to speak the truth now.'

'What truth?' asked Lwando.

'I do not like what our son-in-law is trying to do.'

'What is wrong with taking another wife? Just because you have been my only wife does not mean that your daughter should expect to be her husband's only wife all his life. Polygamy is a Ngoni tradition, whether you and your daughter like it or not.'

'I know it is Ngoni culture, baba. But I do not think your son-in-law wants to take another wife just to follow Ngoni tradition. That son-in-law of yours has been away from Ngoni culture for so long that he does not remember much of it. I think he is up to some trick,' said Mwaziona.

'What trick?'

'Baba, your son-in-law knows that your daughter will not accept living in a polygamous family on account of her Christian beliefs.'

'And so?'

'That is the trick. Your son-in-law does not love your daughter any longer. But he does not want to divorce her for he knows that if he did, he would have no reasons to give the court. All he wants is to provoke your daughter into divorcing him. That way, she would be to blame. If your daughter refuses to live in sin and divorces him, she will lose all her children. She will lose her dignity. We must help her,' said Mwaziona.

'So you agree with me,' Lwando told his wife.

'Agree about what? I do not agree with you.'

'From what you have said, you agree with me. I know that she stands to lose a lot if her marriage breaks up. It does not matter who initiates the divorce. Whether she divorces him or he her, it is your daughter who will suffer. That is why I have told her to remain with her husband whether he decides to take a second wife or not. As long as she remains his wife, he will be duty bound to look after her and all his children. Do you not see the wisdom in what I am saying?'

'No! You are wrong, baba. When he takes another wife, he will no longer look after your daughter well. You must stop him.'

'Have you been listening to your daughter? Those are not your words but hers. As a mother of many children, she must be prepared to suffer a little for their sake.'

Mwaziona kept quiet. She did not want to prolong the discussion lest it developed into an unnecessary argument. But she was not going to let her daughter suffer. She would stand by her.

EIGHT

Musa did not have a house in the village. Since their arrival, they had been accommodated by three different families. That arrangement had suited Musa because he had not expected them to stay long before returning to Southern Rhodesia. But after a while, he thought of a new plan. He would leave Tisa and the children behind and return to V.V.'s farm by himself. Only after his wedding to Rhoda would he send the fare for Tisa and the children to follow. That way, he would have a peaceful wedding.

This prompted him to consider building a house for his family. He was going to make it the biggest house in Nkhanza, with three bedrooms and one living-room. He would build a separate kitchen and two other small houses for the children.

Musa was about to employ men to build the houses when headman Nkhanza heard of it, and prohibited this. Building houses was a communal duty. 'Tell us what sort of houses you want and we will build them,' he told Musa.

When the houses were completed, headman Nkhanza hired a witch-doctor to make them invisible to witches.

Tisa was gradually losing weight due to worry. They had come back to Northern Rhodesia at her request for she had hoped that someone would dissuade her husband from taking a second wife. But it now looked like nobody could do so. Since the day her father had sided with her husband, Tisa had not raised the matter with him again. He would not be moved. She was now hopeless and helpless. Yet she was certain that she would not live happily in a polygamous family. As a Christian, she did not want to live in sin. But even if she were not a Christian, she would not stand a co-wife. She was going to speak to her mother again. Perhaps she had worked out something as she had promised.

One afternoon as he sat on his chair and Tisa on a reed mat at some distance, Musa invited his wife to move closer. Touched by his polite approach, Tisa obliged.

'Something has been on my mind for some time,' he said. 'My leave is coming to an end, but I do not have enough money for all of our fares. I have decided to leave you and the children behind. When I get to Walale, I will send you the fares.'

Tisa did not say anything. Her husband was interested only in his impending marriage to Rhoda. That must be the reason why he was in a hurry to return to Southern Rhodesia.

'What do you think?' Musa asked.

'Nothing.'

'Is that all you can say?'

'What do you expect me to say when you have already decided to go and marry your Rhoda?'

'Tisa, why do you want to be difficult? If I have no money for fares, there is nothing I can do.'

'That is not true. If you cared about us, you would ask V.V. to send you money and he would do so. He has done that in the past each time that you have run out of money whilst here. Let us stop talking about this because it makes my head ache,' said Tisa. 'I do not want to be a co-wife.'

'But you heard what your father said,' Musa told her.

'I will talk to my parents again. When they were here, there was no time for them to hear my story and give the matter serious consideration. Now that they are back home, they will consult other people. When I return, I will have a different response from them.'

'Tisa, my father-in-law is a wise man. He knows that I am right and that you are confused. You are free to go to Mtendere, but it will not help you,' said Musa. And neither of them said another word. Unable to bear the silence, Tisa picked up her reed mat and went to sit in the kitchen.

As soon as she arrived in Mtendere, Tisa discussed the matter with her mother. Mwaziona agreed with her – an effort had to be made to talk her husband out of his plan. Tisa would talk to her father again.

But when Lwando heard what his daughter had come for, he was enraged and told her to return to her husband at once. He further warned everybody in Mtendere against harbouring her and threatened that anyone found lodging her would be charged with trying to break her marriage.

Mwaziona was unhappy with her husband's attitude. If only she could promise her daughter another way out! But if her father said she must go back to her husband, nobody would say anything to the contrary.

Four days later, just after sunset, Tisa was back in Nkhanza. Musa found his wife seated outside the kitchen of their new house.

'How were Father and Mother when you left Mtendere?' he asked after their supper.

'They were all right.'

And then silence descended upon them. The children sat around their mother but did not say anything because of their father's presence. Musa did not take kindly to children making a noise when he was around. He rarely had anything to say to them. In fact, he never wanted their company. There was a great distance between him and his eldest three children. He tolerated the company of his younger sons, Yosefe and Luka, and his youngest daughter, Lute. He saw these three every evening. After supper, he would summon them and assign some task to each of them.

'Yosefe, pull my toes until every one of them produces a cracking sound. Lute, do the same to my fingers. Do not stop until each one of them has produced that sound. Let me hear twenty cracking sounds altogether,' he would tell them. 'And Luka, scratch the bottom of my feet softly. I like the ticklish feeling.'

Those were the only moments when Musa wanted the company of his children. And only the younger children had this privilege. The older ones, Isaki, Maria and Malita, had since graduated from performing these chores just as Luka, Lute and Yosefe would also be retired when they grew older.

That evening he did not want any of his toes or fingers pulled, nor did he want the bottom of his feet tickled. So, the children sat silently until it was time for them to go to bed. After they had retired, Musa spoke to his wife again.

'Tisa, I want to leave for Southern Rhodesia soon. Before that, I need to tell the village elders about my intention to leave you behind. I must also inform them that I am going to take a second wife when I return to Walale. Now, I want to know what message you have brought from my father-in-law regarding my planned marriage.'

'He did not say anything that you do not already know, baba. He says if you want to take another wife, it is up to you.'

'And what do you say?'

'My heart has not changed. Polygamy is sinful.'

'So, what are you going to do about it, then? Don't you see that nobody supports you?' asked Musa.

'I am not on my own. The Lord, my God, is with me. At this moment, I don't know what I am going to do. However, I go solely by faith. I have been praying for the Lord's guidance and I will continue to do so,' said Tisa. When she turned to her husband, he was asleep.

Tisa reviewed what had happened so far. Her husband was right she was on her own. Her mother was on her side but could not do anything without her husband's support. Yes, from an earthly point of view, she was on her own, but the Lord would not abandon her. And even on earth, she was not completely alone. As a child of God, she had brethren in the Church. She would look for the nearest Church and take her problem there.

When Musa told headman Nkhanza that he wanted to take another wife, the headman asked his nduna to summon the elders.

'Where has our kinsman found the woman?' asked one of the elders after the nduna had introduced the topic.

'Baba Manda will answer that question,' the nduna responded.

'Obaba, the young woman is a schoolteacher at the farm where I am foreman in Southern Rhodesia,' said Musa.

Nobody said a word. Sakala, who had asked the first question, broke the silence with another question.

'Did you say the woman you want to marry is in Walale?'

'Yes.'

'Is she a Ngoni woman?'

'No, she is a Shona,' said Musa. That triggered a lot of whispering until the nduna stopped it.

'If nobody wants to say the truth, I will start,' the nduna began. 'We all agree that our kinsman's decision to take a second wife is a wise one. In spite of that, I am not happy with the woman he has chosen. We have heard many unpleasant stories about those women of Walale. They have no regard for our traditions and do not respect people like us who have lived in the village all our lives. Nobody can be happy with Baba Musa's choice.'

'Not a single one of us,' said one man who sat next to Musa. 'We do not trust those women of Walale. We must not allow our kinsman to land himself into that trouble.'

'I agree with obaba Nduna and Sakala,' said Shuzi. 'My brother should not marry that woman. I do not want to have a sister-in-law who will bring misery into our family. He should look for the right woman whilst he is here.'

'Obaba,' said headman Nkhanza, 'we have heard what our brothers have said. Now, I would like us to hear what Baba Musa thinks about it.'

'There is nothing wrong with women of Walale. They are just as good as our own women, in some cases, even better,' said Musa.

'That is not true,' the nduna interjected.

'Please, let me finish,' Musa pleaded. 'I have lived in Walale for the past sixteen years. I know the women there are not bad. And Rhoda, the girl whom I want to marry, is a polite person who respects African traditions. Give her a chance . . .'

'Obaba,' headman Nkhanza broke the silence, 'there is one thing which nobody has asked our kinsman. Does mother of Isaki approve of the woman you want to marry?'

'Tisa does not want me to take another wife,' said Musa.

'What!' exclaimed headman Nkhanza. 'Since when did women begin to tell their husbands how many wives they can have? Does Baba Lwando know this?'

'Yes. I told him when he came for my vipheko.'

'What did he say?'

'He said that as a Ngoni, I am free to take as many wives as I can afford.'

'True! Tisa has no right to dictate to you. She must be ashamed of herself,' said headman Nkhanza. 'My second question is this: Have you already put Tisa and that second wife-to-be of yours on the same mat to shake hands?'

'No. Is that necessary?' Musa asked.

'Absolutely! How can you bring two women into your household if they hate each other so much that they cannot shake hands or share the same mat?'

'What if one of them refuses to co-operate?' asked Musa.

'It is your responsibility to ensure that the women you intend to bring together are compatible. It seems you have not done all that a man who wants to be a polygamist is supposed to do. The only advice we can give you now is that you give this whole issue another thought. If you still want to have two wives, make sure you are able to bring your first wife and the one you intend to marry to sit on the same mat and shake hands. Only then can you start to involve us,' the headman told Musa. 'If anybody has anything else to say, obaba, let him say it now.'

Nobody spoke.

'Baba Musa,' said headman Nkhanza, 'what we are telling you is that you must make sure that you have made the right choice before you rush into your intended second marriage. Thank you, obaba, for having come to advise our brother. Go in peace!'

Tisa discovered the nearest Dutch Reformed Church two villages away from Nkhanza. It was a humble congregation where services were held in the open air under fig trees. It was known as the Katawa Congregation after the nearest stream in the area. That congregation did not have a pastor. Occasionally, one visited them from Nsadzu Mission. Sometimes, a different pastor came from Madzimoyo. Once every three months, the whole congregation walked twelve miles to either Nsadzu or Madzimoyo on a Saturday in order to be on time for the service the following day. Such were the only occasions when they would partake of the holy Communion.

The congregation was under the leadership of two men, both from humble backgrounds. Neither of them had received any formal education but had been taught how to read and write in Cinyanja. Tisa took all of her seven children with her on her first Sunday to the Katawa Congregation. Their welcome was tremendous. One of the two elders, whose name she later learnt was Mwanza, introduced her and her children to the congregation.

Tisa was happy and praised the Lord. She was sure she would find good fellowship there. It would be the right place to take her sorrows and her joys from then on.

Musa did not reveal the exact date of his departure to anyone until the evening before he was due to leave. Even his wife did not know. Later, he explained to her that it would be unsafe to announce his departure in advance. Everyone knew the risks involved, he told her. If a person leaving for Walale made the date of his departure public, that person was actually inviting witches to visit him. It was safer to keep the departure date a secret. That way, the witches would have no time to prepare their deadly medicines for the departing person.

He left the village at dawn. He did not want to be seen leaving. Tisa volunteered to see him off to the bus-stop but he dissuaded her.

NINE

Travelling back to Southern Rhodesia, Musa set out his priorities. On arrival, the first person he would see was V.V. and the second, Rhoda. The most important matters on his mind were his job and his bride. Anything else could wait.

Once back, he found his home dead silent. This made him rush the marriage. When the day arrived, it was a big occasion. V.V. had declared it a holiday, slaughtered three bulls and made two lorries available to ferry invited guests from neighbouring farms. Everybody at the farm, even Banda and his wife, attended the celebration.

After the wedding, Rhoda moved into Musa's two-bedroom house. It was the only two-bedroom house at the farm. Up to now, this house and his three huts had been adequate for Musa. Now that he had acquired another wife, he would need more room. Tisa would never agree to live under the same roof as her co-wife. If he approached V.V., he would build him another two-bedroom house.

Tisa prayed daily for her marriage. She wished her husband would write and tell her that he was not going to marry Rhoda. Two months after his departure a letter arrived from him. As she tore the envelope open, her fingers shook with anxiety.

V.V. Farm, P.O. Trelawney, S.R.
3-6-1956

Dear Mother of Isaki,

How are the children?

I am pleased to let you know that your co-wife is now home. The marriage took place a week ago.

I have not sent you the fares because there is a problem which I must sort out before you come. Now that there are two of you, we will need another house. V.V. has promised to make one available. When the house is ready, I will send you the money.

I am your husband of all times,
Musandivute.

Tisa wondered what she would do next. Since she started
attending services at Katawa, she had put off telling the Church
elders about her marital problems. Now she was going to tell
them. They could not make her husband nullify his sinful
marriage, but they would console her and encourage her to
remain strong in her faith. Perhaps it would be proper to inform
Shuzi and the headman before taking the matter to Church.

'Mother of Isaki,' said headman Nkhanza, 'I do not want to bite
my tongue. What you have told me is bad. A man should build a
house before he takes a wife. You must tell Shuzi about this.'

Tisa informed Shuzi that evening.

'Do not worry,' said Shuzi. 'You can wait in this village for as
long as it takes my brother to find a house.' Shuzi wished his
sister-in-law would stay in the village indefinitely. He saw
advantages in looking after his brother's family. His brother had
four sons. That would give him four herdboys for his cattle.
There were also three daughters. It would be his responsibility to
charge cimalo and malowolo for those girls' marriages. The
cattle would go into his kraal.

One Sunday, Tisa told the leaders of the Katawa congregation
about her marital problems. Agreeing that it was a serious
problem, they decided to study one Corinthians, chapter seven
where guidelines on Christian marriage were found. Tisa was
pleased that they had chosen that chapter for it contained her
favourite verses.

When they had gone through the whole chapter, Tisa read
verses ten and eleven aloud all over again:

*To the married I give this command (not I, but the
Lord): A wife must not separate from her husband.
But if she does, she must remain unmarried or else be
reconciled to her husband. And a husband must not
divorce his wife.*

'Praise God for those consoling verses,' said one elder. 'Let us add verses thirteen, fifteen and sixteen to your favourites,' he suggested and began to read:

And if a woman has a husband who is not a
believer and he is willing to live with her, she must
not divorce him. But if the unbeliever leaves, let
him do so. A believing man or woman is not
bound in such circumstances; God has called us to
live in peace.
   How do you know, wife, whether you will save your
husband? Or, how do you know, husband, whether
you will save your wife?

'Our sister,' said one elder, 'we will pray for you until a solution is found to this problem. Before we depart, let us bow our heads in prayer.' And he prayed for Tisa.

A month after Musa's wedding, V.V. offered him an extra house. It was a three-bedroom house with electricity, running water, a toilet and bathroom. It had previously belonged to V.V.'s son, who, having graduated from the University of Rhodesia and Nyasaland, was leaving the farm to become a schoolteacher.

Moving into that house enhanced Musa's authority, but two things bothered him. Firstly, there was no longer any reason not to send Tisa the fares. Secondly, who, between Tisa and Rhoda, was entitled to a bigger house? One of his wives had to accept the two-bedroom house. He wished he could leave it to them to decide.

'Rhoda,' he began, 'I have to send money to Northern Rhodesia for Tisa and the children to join us.'

'Yes?'

'But there is one problem. I do not know which of you should live in the old house,' he told her.

Rhoda considered the matter. She did not want to move back to the two-bedroom house. What would people think of her if she did?

'Would you mind moving back into the old house?' he asked.

'Do you want me to?' asked Rhoda.

'I don't know.'

'You know something,' said Rhoda, 'as a polygamist, never let your wives take decisions which affect them.'

Musa did not raise that matter again.

The second letter from her husband arrived two months after the first. It did not excite her. Tisa did not expect good news.

10-8-1956

Dear Mother of Isaki,

How are the children? Rhoda and I are fine. V.V. has given me another house. I will send you the fares soon.

I am your husband of all times,

Musandivute.

Tisa wondered why he had written the letter. Since returning to Southern Rhodesia, he had received two salaries. Why had he failed to send her the money? And V.V. had given him another house. He had no excuse for keeping her waiting.

She was going to answer his letter and tell him what was on her mind. She would also ask the headman for a piece of land where she could grow her own food. If she was to remain in the village indefinitely, it would be unwise to sit idle.

15-8-1956

Dear Father of Isaki,

Since you do not want to send any money for our bus fare, you must send us food. Send mealie meal, beans, groundnuts, sugar, salt, cooking oil, bath soap and washing-powder.

I am your wife,

Tisauke.

During the weeks that followed, Chief Sairi the Third sent a special message to Chief Nzamane the Second. He wanted help from his fellow chief. In Chief Sairi's village, there was a primary school. The chief loved that school and did not want it to collapse. But there was a problem that year. The headmaster had failed to find forty children for the year's intake. He was asking Chief Nzamane to persuade his people to send their children to that school.

Chief Nzamane dispatched his kaphasos from village to village in search of children of school-going age. That search yielded no results. People in Chief Nzamane's area did not want to send their children to school. They wanted their sons to look after cattle until they reached the age of sixteen. Thereafter, they were expected to graduate into ploughing their fathers' fields until they were about eighteen. Between the age of eighteen and twenty, society required them to find themselves wives. Those who remained single long after their twentieth birthday were viewed with a mixture of suspicion and sympathy.

The situation for girls was not very different. Before they came of age, they were required to assist their mothers with the day-to-day chores of the home. When they came of age, their parents looked forward to the day when they would get married.

This displeased the two chiefs. They resolved to use some amount of coercion for the people to release their children. They sent out a combined force of kaphasos from their two courts with orders to round up all boys and girls of school-going age. This plan, however, was leaked to one or two ordinary folk who allowed it to spread freely. As a result, many families hid their children from public sight during the period.

Meanwhile, Tisa decided that her sons, Isaki and Yosefe, should be recruited. But her plans were opposed by her brother-in-law. Shuzi was not going to let the boys go. He wanted them to look after cattle like normal Ngoni boys. He ordered that when the chief's kaphasos come, the two boys must go into the forest and hide with other boys until it was safe to return.

Tisa appealed to the headman who advised that at least one boy be allowed to go to school. He, however, cautioned Tisa that she had no right to do anything without her brother-in-law's blessing. He further ruled that Shuzi should decide which of the two boys went to school. Tisa accepted the compromise, and

Shuzi decided that Isaki should go to school. Yosefe would have to start looking after cattle.

By mid-August of 1956, Isaki was a pupil at Sairi Lower Primary School. He spent only one year there. The school provided tuition for Sub A, Sub B, and Standards One and Two. For Standard Three, one moved to an upper school where only those who passed Standard Two well earned a place.

Having started Standard Two at V.V.'s farm school, Isaki joined Sairi straight into Standard Two as a repeater. In the Standard Two examinations, his performance was so impressive that it earned him a handshake with Chief Sairi. Out of a class of forty, only four boys and one girl were selected for Standard Three. Isaki and the other three successful boys were to move to Angoni Upper Primary Boarding School.

But the school was not free. The annual fees were nine pounds and fifteen shillings. Isaki's mother could not raise that money. The only option was to write to her husband. She had not written to him for some time. She had not seen any reason to do so for he had given her false promises. Now that she needed money for Isaki's fees, she had to write to him. She agreed with Isaki that he should write to his father himself.

16th May, 1957

My dear father,

How are you? Here, we are all fine.

Last year, I started Standard Two at Sairi Primary School. I have now qualified for Standard Three at a boarding school. The fees are nine pounds and fifteen shillings. I beg you to send this money urgently. I have to report at the school on 7 August.

I have written this letter alone. I can now read and write well in Cinyanja. I also know a few English words.

I am your beloved son,

Isaki.

Isaki awaited his father's response for more than two months until he began to panic. When he talked to his mother, they agreed to ask Shuzi for help, two days before schools opened.

'Nine pounds and fifteen shillings is a lot of money,' said Shuzi. 'Isaki must stop school. Those are my words.'

The day before he was due to report at school, Isaki decided that he would go to Angoni with or without fees. He recalled his mother's words of faith. She had told him that nothing was impossible for the Lord. That night, he packed his belongings in readiness for his walk to school. His baggage consisted of two paper bags. In one bag, he put one of his two pairs of uniforms from Sairi School. He would wear the other pair. In the second bag, he carried a whole smoked chicken, fried groundnuts, roasted sweet potatoes and a tin of home-made groundnut paste.

At the school, Isaki saw a queue in front of one building. He learnt that the queue was for new boys waiting for the headmaster. Each boy had a suitcase beside him. With his two paper bags in either hand, he joined the queue, and eyes turned on him. Then some audible whispering about him began, but Isaki worried more about what the headmaster would say.

He closed his eyes and said a short prayer. 'Our Father in heaven, help me explain my plight clearly to the headmaster. And please, Lord, make him understand my circumstances. I ask this in the name of my Lord and Saviour, Jesus Christ, Amen!'

The boys continued whispering and chattering for some time until a tall fat man was spotted walking towards them. At the sight of this man, the chattering faded away. As the man approached, some boys whispered, 'That's our headmaster!'

Suddenly, there was total silence. The headmaster walked past them and, without a word, unlocked the door of his office and closed it behind him. He remained there for what seemed like infinite time. That made the boys resume whispering. The whispering changed to chattering and the chattering to ear-splitting noise. At first, the headmaster tolerated it but when it began to sound like an outright commotion, he burst out of his office and yelled at them.

'Where do you think you are?' he roared. 'Keep quiet or I'll send you back to lower primary school to repeat Standard Two until you grow a little older.'

Dead silence followed and the headmaster went back into his office. Isaki wished the boys had not angered him.

The headmaster emerged from his office, stood in front of the boys and stared at them. Time and again, he frowned in such a way that the wrinkles on his forehead moved about like waves in a rough stream. That scared even the bravest of the boys. Isaki wondered if he was right to come when he had no money.

'Welcome to Angoni Upper School,' he told them. 'I'm your headmaster. One of the things I hate is being made angry by a pupil. What sort of things make me angry? There are twenty of them. I have them all written down here,' he said, pulling a piece of paper from his notebook. 'We call them school rules. You'll find a copy of these rules on notice-boards. Read them carefully,' he said and paused.

'One rule which starts to apply here and now is this: "Do not speak vernacular between ten o'clock on Sunday evening and five o'clock in the afternoon on Friday." This means that between those days and times, no Cicewa or Cingoni or Cinsenga or Cikunda or Citumbuka must be heard in this school. During those times, you are expected to speak English. If you do not know any English, keep your mouth shut until the weekend.

'I want to see each of you, one at a time. In my office, produce your acceptance letter and nine pounds and fifteen shillings. Before showing me the letter and the money, tell me the name of your previous school and then your name and your father's. When I get the money, I'll give you a receipt. You'll then proceed to the food store where the boarding-master is waiting for you. You'll show him your receipt and he will issue you with bedding and tell you to which house you belong. Are there any questions?'

Nobody said a word. Isaki was now perspiring from worry.

'Next!' the headmaster shouted.

It was his turn to go in. Once in front of the headmaster, he placed his paper bags on the floor and stood at attention. The headmaster looked at him from toes to hair.

'What are you supposed to say?' the headmaster asked him.

'I am sorry, sir,' Isaki began and the headmaster sat up. This boy could speak English! That attracted his attention.

'I have not brought any money, sir,' Isaki continued.

'You haven't?' the headmaster asked. 'What is your story?'

'My father is in Southern Rhodesia. I sent a letter to him in May and asked him for the money but he has not answered.'

'When do you think he will send the money?'

'I don't know, sir.'

The headmaster eyed the boy all over again from his bare feet to his head, and then to his two paper bags.

'Where is your suitcase?'

'I don't have a suitcase, sir.'

'Where are your belongings?' the headmaster asked him again and Isaki pointed at his paper bags.

'Is that all you have?'

'Yes, sir?'

'What's your name?'

'Isaki Manda.'

'Which lower primary school are you from?'

'Sairi, sir.'

The headmaster turned to his notebook and flipped through its pages. And then he nodded his head positively.

'Isaki, I'm sending all those without fees back home and I don't want them to return without the money. However, in your case, I won't send you home because you say your father is in Southern Rhodesia. I want you to write to him again. Tell him that you have already started Standard Three and that he must send the money directly to me. If we do not receive the money from him within the next five weeks, we will send you away.'

The headmaster wrote the address of the school on a piece of paper and gave it to Isaki.

'Tell your father to send the money to me at this address,' the headmaster told him and began to write a note which he said to take to the boarding-master.

The boarding-master read through the note once and then turned to the bearer whom he eyed from bare feet to head. Then he went back to the note and read it a second time:

To the boarding-master:

Please issue the bearer with his bedding and mug. His father will send the fees from Southern Rhodesia.

Headmaster.

'So your father is in Southern Rhodesia?' he asked Isaki.

'Yes, sir.'

'Why did he not send you the money on time?'

'I don't know, sir,' said Isaki. And the boarding-master took another look at him from toes to hair before he decided to give him the blankets and a mug marked N.R.G., which stood for Northern Rhodesia Government.

TEN

Musa had not written to Tisa for a year. He did not know what to write to her about. In her last letter, she had offended him by asking him to send her foodstuff. He decided not to write to her until she wrote to him again. But Tisa did not write for months. The next letter was from his son, Isaki. That letter took him by surprise. He had not been told that his son had resumed school. Instead, he got a request for boarding fees. How was he expected to send nine pounds and fifteen shillings at no notice? That was almost his entire monthly salary.

Something else bothered him. He had received another letter from Isaki informing him that he had been admitted at school on condition that he sent the fees directly to the headmaster. He did not like that. He was sure that Tisa was playing tricks. She must have given that idea to the headmaster. He had to put a stop to her tricks.

23-9-1957

Dear Mother of Isaki,

How are the children?

I am angry that you put Isaki in school without consulting me. Why did you do that when you knew that my plans were to send you money so that you would join us? You told Isaki to ask me for school fees. If you knew you had no money, why did you have him enrolled in school?

While I was still agonising about Isaki's first letter, you told his headmaster that I would pay the money within five weeks. That headmaster did not have to know that the father of Isaki was in Southern Rhodesia. If you need money for anything, write directly to me yourself.

With regard to your travel here, I am not sending you the money. I would like to take leave and come there. When I do, we will sort out all these problems.

I am your husband of all times,
Musandivute.

Isaki waited for his father's response. The headmaster of the school also waited for the fees. But neither of them heard from him. When the five weeks which the headmaster had given Isaki expired, the boy began to hope that the headmaster would forget about it, but he did not. On the day that the five weeks expired, he summoned all those boys who had not paid the fees.

When he entered the office, Isaki lost even the little hope he had for he saw Mr Zulu, the boarding-master, seated next to the headmaster. He feared the former more than he did the latter. He was not the only one who dreaded him. In the dormitories, the mere mention of his name would immediately paralyse every-one.

Isaki stood at attention. For some time, neither of the men looked at him. Mr Ndlovu, the headmaster, kept on studying his notebook whilst Mr Zulu looked on from a little distance.

'What's your name?' the headmaster asked him.

'Isaki Manda,' said Mr Zulu. 'How much is he owing?'

'Everything,' said Mr Ndlovu. 'This is the boy whose father is in Southern Rhodesia.'

'Do you believe that, Mr Ndlovu?'

'Why not?'

'Is your father in Walale?' Mr Zulu asked Isaki.

'Yes, sir.'

'That is a lie. Do you think you can fool us? If you have no father, say so,' Mr Zulu told him.

Isaki did not know what to say. For a moment, he wished he had no father. Perhaps if he had no father, these men would have helped him.

'What does your father do in Southern Rhodesia?' the headmaster asked.

'He is a farm foreman, sir.'

'That is a good job,' said the headmaster. 'I am sure he can afford to send us the fees.'

'Does your father know that we need this money?' the boarding-master asked.

'Yes, sir. I have sent him two letters.'

'What has he said?' the boarding-master continued.

'He has not answered my letters, sir.'

A variety of thoughts went through Isaki's mind. One moment, he wished they would tell him to go home for good. He detested the interrogation he was going through. The next moment, he prayed, asking the Lord to soften the hearts of the two men.

'Where is your mother?' the headmaster asked.

'At home, sir.'

The headmaster looked at him from his toes to his hair.

'Go out and wait till we call you in again,' he told Isaki.

When they had attended to all the boys who had been waiting outside, they reviewed Isaki's position and struck a compromise. They were going to send him home whilst they investigated whether he had a father and if so, whether it was true that he was employed in Southern Rhodesia. If they discovered that the boy had no father, they would not interrogate him any further. Instead, they would summon him back to school and find ways in which they could assist him.

Back in the office, neither of them asked him any questions. The headmaster spoke solemnly.

'Isaki, we believe what you have told us,' the headmaster began. 'We also know that you're brilliant. For that reason, we want you to continue with school. Unfortunately, the Government can't allow us to keep you here when you haven't paid the fees. However, we're sending you back home to ask your mother to write to your father again. She should tell him that we'll keep your place for three weeks. As soon as you receive the money, you may return. If he has no money to send just yet, he must write a letter promising to send the money. Is that clear?'

'Yes, sir.'

Isaki arrived home at sunset with his paper bags.

'Do not tell me, my child. They have chased you from school because of the money,' said Tisa. 'What shall we do now?'

'I have not been expelled, mother. The headmaster said we should write to my father and ask him to send the money. I wrote to him when I got to school but he has not answered.'

'I know that, my child. He sent the reply to me.'

'What did he say?'

'Nothing. Read the letter for yourself,' she said, handing him the letter.

'Is my father all right these days?' asked Isaki.

'That is the question I have been asking myself for a long time, my child,' said Tisa.

'What shall we do?'

'We must pray,' she told him. 'Our Lord Jesus Christ told us that whatever we asked in his name, God would provide.'

For two days, they did not raise the matter. Then Tisa decided to go and discuss the problem about her husband with her father. On the fourth day, Tisa and Isaki departed for Mtendere.

That evening, Lwando asked Tisa what they had come for.

'Is it well where you have come from?' he enquired.

'It is well, baba, for nobody is ill. But I cannot say that all is truly well.'

'What is troubling your heart, mother of Isaki?'

'It is your son-in-law, baba. I do not know what is going on in his heart. When he left us last year, he said he would send me money for our journey back to Walale as soon as he arrived. But up to this day, he has not done so.'

'The problem is that I need money for school,' interrupted Isaki. 'The headmaster of Angoni has given me three weeks in which to find nine pounds and fifteen shillings. Please help me.'

'Isaki, you must learn to wait until elders finish speaking. Is that what they teach you at school?' Lwando complained. 'Keep quiet until your mother has finished talking to me.'

'That is the story, baba, but I have not come for money. I only want you to know what your son-in-law is doing. He has abandoned me and the children.'

'Those are words, baba,' Mwaziona told her husband.

'Yes, mother of Isaki, those are words. But there is nothing we can do because we have only heard it from you. You must go back and take your grievances to headman Nkhanza and your brother-in-law. Ask them to bring the problem to me. As soon as I am properly informed by them, I will consider the matter. As it

is, let us assume that I do not know anything,' Lwando concluded and then bade his daughter and grandson good night.

But Mwaziona raised the matter again.

'It is a problem, but there is nothing I can do,' Lwando insisted. 'If Tisa has problems with her husband, she must complain
to his people. We must follow tradition.'

'Baba, I know what Ngoni customs say. But Tisa's situation is
unique in that the real problem is not her husband but the foreign
woman he has married there in Walale. She is dangerous.'

'Do not get carried away by your emotions,' Lwando advised
his wife. 'You and I are nearing the end of our lives. Tisa has a
whole life ahead of her. She has children to bring up and those
children will have children to bring up and so on. Let us not
cause her to destroy her family. We must help her build it even if
it means doing so from ruins.'

'That will not do. Our son-in-law wants our child to give up
waiting for him. He thinks she will eventually misbehave with
another man. That way, he would take her and the man to court
where he would be compensated and allowed to divorce Tisa.
The courts would further rule that he takes all the children. Yes,
our days are numbered. That is why we must ensure that our
daughter's problem is sorted out whilst we live.'

A moment of silence followed. When Mwaziona next said
something, her husband was softly snoring.

The headmaster of Angoni Upper School established that Isaki
had a father and that he was, indeed, employed as a foreman at a
tobacco farm in Southern Rhodesia. In spite of that, the
headmaster was convinced that Isaki was no better than
someone without a father. According to his sources, Isaki's
father had abandoned his mother and all her children. For that
reason, the school decided to find him a bursary.

Eventually, he was awarded the Angoni Native Authority
bursary which would initially be for two years. Thereafter, it
would be reviewed. Its renewal would depend on his
performance in the middle school-leaving examinations which
he was to take at the end of Standard Four.

The following year, Isaki passed the middle school-leaving examinations well and his bursary was renewed for a further two years. After those two years, the bursary would not be renewed.

'It is a pity that the Angoni Native Authority does not award any bursaries for secondary school,' the headmaster told him. 'Otherwise, we would have recommended you highly for another renewal. I am confident that you will do equally well in your upper school-leaving examinations next year.'

When he returned to Angoni Upper School for Standard Five, Isaki wrote to his father.

Angoni Upper School, P.O. Kazimule, Northern Rhodesia.
30th May, 1959.

My dear father,

How are you? Here we are all well.

I am glad to let you know that I am still in school. Two years ago, I had been sent away from school for lack of fees. However, the Lord provided the required amount of money.

I am now in Standard Five. This year too, the Lord has made it possible for me to continue schooling. Last year, I sat for the Standard Four examinations and passed with high marks. If it should please our Father in heaven, I will be completing my primary school next year. I hope to pass the Standard Six examinations and qualify for secondary school. Please, Baba, may I know when you will come home to see us?

I send you my greetings in the name of our Lord and Saviour, Jesus Christ.

I am your beloved child,
Isaki.

He looked forward to his father's reply. He needed to hear how happy he was about his success at school. But the whole of the first term, Isaki did not receive a letter from his father. At the beginning of the second term, he sent his father his fourth letter. But that term also came to an end. He decided that when he went home for the school holidays at the end of Standard Five, he would take stock of his family's situation and write to his father about that. Perhaps baba was beginning to forget them. Maybe a detailed letter about each one of them would remind him of their existence.

When he got home, he learnt that his two elder sisters were due to wed. His father had given his consent through letters. They were going to be married in the Dutch Reformed Church in the same month. Maria would marry first and three weeks later, Malita would follow. The men who were marrying them were both employed in the mines on the Copperbelt. The marriages had been arranged through correspondence. The men, both from the Fort Jameson district, did not want to marry girls from the Copperbelt. Like many other young men from Fort Jameson, they believed that girls born and bred in the Copperbelt towns did not make good wives.

When Isaki came home for the school holidays, this was the news he found. His mother briefed him about the marriages.

'Is my father coming for the weddings?' Isaki asked.

'No, my child. We asked him to attend but he said V.V. could not do without him at the farm. Perhaps one day, your brothers-in-law might take leave from the mines and pay him a visit with your sisters. Maybe that is what your father needs now. Those who want to see him might have to follow him to where he is. I have given up. I will wait in this village until the day he decides to send me back to Mtendere. Perhaps that is what he is planning to do.

'I do not mind what he thinks of me any more. I only want to bring you all up well so that in future you may look after me. Work hard at school in order to get a good job. God knows why all this is happening to us. As His Word teaches us, let us not fix our eyes on those things that are seen but rather on those that are not visible, for what is seen is temporary whilst what is unseen is eternal. That is what we read in two Corinthians chapter four, verse eighteen. That Word is a great source of encouragement to me. I urge you to study it too.'

Now that he knew his father had been in touch with his

family, Isaki changed his mind about writing to him. From what his mother had told him, there was nothing that his father did not know about the family. If his daughters' weddings did not excite him and make him come to Nkhanza, Isaki did not think anything else could. Like his mother, he would merely wait until his father decided to communicate. For the time being, he would take everyone's advice seriously. He would concentrate only on his studies. That was what his mother had urged him to do and that was what his teachers had advised him, too.

ELEVEN

In the first week of July, 1960, Isaki went back to Angoni Upper School for his final year, determined to work hard. He did not want to let his mother and his teachers down. Above all, he was not going to let the Lord down. His mother had told him that as a child of God, he had to bear in mind that whatever he did, he should do it for the Lord. He remembered the scripture from Colossians chapter three, verses twenty-three and twenty-four:

> *Whatever you do, work at it with all your heart,*
> *as working for the Lord, not for men, since you*
> *know that you will receive an inheritance from the*
> *Lord as a reward.*

He had two examinations coming up in the same year. He would take the secondary school entrance examinations, followed by the upper school-leaving examinations. In order to qualify for secondary school, one had to pass both examinations well. Getting a place in secondary school was not an easy matter but he was determined to do so. In the past, not more than three boys from Angoni had ever been selected for secondary school. In the previous year, only two people had been selected for Form One. But that did not scare him. Even if they selected only one boy from his school, it would be him. He had a great deal of faith in God.

Then came the last day of that academic year. A government Landrover had been spotted at the headmaster's office the day before. That sparked off a rumour that the vehicle had brought the Standard Six results. But nobody could confirm that rumour. The headmaster had kept the news as his own secret.

On the last day of the year, Standard Six boys sat in the front part of the assembly hall. They were followed by the Standard Threes, the Standard Fours and the Standard Fives. As they waited for the headmaster and the rest of the staff to come into the hall, the heart of every Standard Six pounded with anxiety. Even Isaki was nervous. For the first time, he felt that failing the examinations was a possibility.

He had done his best in both examinations, but anything could happen. He had heard of brilliant people failing on account of their having misread the questions. Or the examiners could have made an error. What if they gave his marks to some dull chap and gave him that other boy's marks? There would be no way of finding out that mistake.

In the hall, while the Standard Sixes sat quietly, the rest of the school sang farewell songs to them. Standard Sixes would reciprocate. One song that every Standard Six class sang at the end of the year was entitled 'No more'. The Standard Sixes would sing this song several times and so loudly that even the teachers who would be holding their end-of-year staff meeting would receive the message clearly.

Traditionally, that song was meant for both the remaining pupils and the staff. It was partly meant to tease those teachers who the school-leavers felt had been mean and strict. Some teachers did not like the song. It offended them. But the 1961 school-leavers seemed atypical. They did not sing that song. Normally, the Standard Sixes made sure that they sang this song most loudly as the teachers walked into the assembly hall.

When the headmaster and staff walked in, all the pupils stood at attention in total silence, and the hearts of the Standard Sixes pounded fiercely. As they froze at attention, they wondered who the lucky few would be that year. The school had always produced three boys or fewer for secondary school. In some years, none of the three were for Chizongwe Secondary School. The previous year, only two had been selected for secondary school and neither of them had been selected for Chizongwe.

All the boys were anxious to hear the results. Even those who were not in Standard Six were interested for the results would give them an indication of what the following year's results would be like. But the headmaster did not say a word. He did not even greet the school. He stood silently on the stage and stared menacingly at the Standard Sixes. Then, all of a sudden, he began to sing and the rest of the school – rather startled – joined him:

> No more, no more!
> No more back again.
> No more, no more!
> No more back again.
>
> Whether I fail or pass!
> No more back again.
> Whether I fail or pass!
> No more back again.

By the end of the song, the atmosphere in the hall had brightened up. The Standard Sixes had become a little relaxed after the singing. And the headmaster made things lighter too for he was no longer staring menacingly. Instead, he smiled at them. When he spoke, he addressed the Standard Fives.

'Tell me how many boys you think have qualified for secondary school this year,' he challenged them.

'Three!' some shouted.

'No!' he told them.

'Two!'

'No!'

'One!'

'Wrong!'

'Four!'

'Wrong again!' said the headmaster with pride. 'I'll tell you the answer. But first, here are this year's upper school-leaving examination results,' he continued. Total silence descended upon the entire assembly hall.

'Out of the forty boys who took the exam, all forty have passed,' he announced, and the whole school broke into wild jubilation. Some hit the dining tables while some clapped their hands. Others gave the cement floor of the hall a merciless bang with their mostly bare feet. The headmaster started singing the 'No more' chorus again. This time, everyone joined in.

No more, no more!
No more back again.
No more, no more!
No more back again.

Whether I fail or pass!
No more back again.
Whether I fail or pass!
No more back again.

'And here now are the secondary school entrance exam results,' the headmaster resumed after the song. Many of the Standard Six boys were already smiling with satisfaction. Not all of them expected to go on to secondary school. Some of them knew they could not pass the secondary school entrance examination. These had only been praying that they pass the upper school-leaving examination. Some of them felt that they were too old to continue schooling. Indeed, some of the boys were not really boys. They were men, with wives and a child or two at home.

In those days, most boys did not start school until they were about fourteen as they first had to look after cattle. By the time they took the upper primary school-leaving examination, they were twenty-two years or older. After Standard Six, they could go to college or straight into a civil service job. With the upper primary school-leaving certificate, they could go to a teacher-training college and train to be lower primary schoolteachers within two years. Or they could go to police training school where they could pass out as constables in three months. Or they could join the army and be moulded into disciplined privates in seven months. Some could become medical assistants, others agricultural assistants and so on. Those who were spiritually inclined could be trained as pastors. The job opportunities for a person holding the upper primary school-leaving certificate were not few. So, all in all, the 1961 leavers of Angoni Upper School would all be taken care of since every one of them would receive their certificate. And the headmaster had good news for those whose designs were to go on to secondary school.

'This year, four boys have been accepted for Form One at Chizongwe Secondary School, six at Chasa and six at Katete,' the headmaster announced again. And more shouting and jumping about followed. Thereafter, the headmaster read out the names of the sixteen potential secondary school students.

'This is a record result,' he declared. 'Standard Fives, that is a challenge to you. We expect you to break this record next year. To all our school-leavers, I wish to congratulate you warmly for a job well done. And to the sixteen who are going to secondary school, I say, continue to work hard so that you may put Angoni on the map. You will each receive your acceptance letter from the principal of your secondary school during the holidays. When you get the letter, study it carefully. It will contain a lot of information about the school and all its requirements. You will be told what the fees will be and what things you must take with you. Finally, continue to be as disciplined as you have been here. May God be with you all,' the headmaster concluded.

Isaki was among the four boys who qualified for a place at the coveted Chizongwe Secondary School. But as he walked out of the hall, he was not as excited as his colleagues were. For him, the happiness had been a momentary affair. He was given a place at Chizongwe, but would he find the fees? The Angoni Native Authority had made it clear that their bursaries did not cover secondary school. He wondered what his mother would suggest.

Once they were out of the hall, the school-leavers continued singing the 'No more' song. They sang 'No more' as they walked towards their dormitories to pack up their belongings. They sang 'No more' while they packed and they sang 'No more' all the way to their villages. But Isaki was no longer singing. He had participated in the singing only when the headmaster led the whole school in the song. Now he did not see any reason for rejoicing. Only one thing consoled him – his faith in the Lord. Looking back to when he first arrived at Angoni four years before, he recalled that he did not know whether he would be admitted into Standard Three. But he had prayed for God's assistance. The headmaster and the boarding-master had helped him get a bursary. He had to go and thank them again now that he was leaving the school.

The headmaster was talking to teachers outside his office. Isaki did not want to interrupt them. He stood at attention until one of the teachers – his class teacher – talked to him.

'Do you want to see the headmaster?'

'Yes, sir.'

'What do you want me for, Isaki?' the headmaster asked.

'I came to thank you for helping me, sir. When I came to this school, I did not think I would be admitted for I had no money. May the Lord bless you, sir, and all the teachers.'

The headmaster shook hands with him.

'Well done, my boy!' he congratulated him. 'You did well in both exams. When you go to Chizongwe, work hard. You have a bright future. By the way, what would you like to be when you complete school?' the headmaster asked him.

For the first time since he started school, Isaki realised that he had never thought of a career.

'I don't know, sir. I have never thought about that.'

'Well, I will suggest a career for you,' the headmaster told him. 'You must work hard to become a medical doctor. I know you can make it. When you go to Chizongwe, work hard in your science subjects. In order to train as a doctor, you will have to pass Form Six and then go on to university. There, you will study for quite a few years. I am not sure exactly how many years but I know you will make it because you have the will and discipline to succeed.

'You have three more exams before you qualify for university. The first will be the junior secondary school-leaving exam, the second your "O" level exams in Form Five and the final one will be the "A" levels at the end of Form Six. For Form Six, you should go to Munali High School in Lusaka. After Form Six, you will need to go to the University of Rhodesia and Nyasaland in Salisbury. It is a long way to go but you can make it. You are still young,' the headmaster advised him.

'I will do my best, sir,' Isaki promised and then bade the headmaster and the teachers farewell. He was the last boy to leave Angoni that day. All his way home, he wondered how he would become a medical doctor when he did not know where his next school fees were coming from.

TWELVE

Isaki arrived home thinking about the career advice he had been given by his headmaster. He wondered how long it would take him to qualify as a doctor. He would work hard to pass all his school exams. If other people before him had passed them, why shouldn't he? After clearing 'A' levels, he would proceed to the University of Rhodesia and Nyasaland in Southern Rhodesia. Maybe during his studies there, he would be re-united with his father who would be proud to have a child in university. When Isaki had rested, he told his mother about his examination success.

'That is good, my child. Let us praise the Lord for that,' said his mother. 'You can now go to college, is it not so?'

'Yes, mama. Or I could go to Fort Jameson and ask for a job in any government office or in a private company. They would take me because I passed well.'

'Have you thought of what type of job you want?'

'No. I am still thinking about that,' said Isaki.

'Have you ever thought of serving the Lord?'

'Serving the Lord? What do you mean?'

'The priest at Madzimoyo asked me if you would like to train as a pastor after Standard Six. He said they could train you there. They have a school for priests.'

Isaki considered the proposal. Becoming a priest had never crossed his mind. Working for the Lord would be a satisfying experience. But should he abandon his studies? He was not going to lose the opportunity to go to Chizongwe Secondary School. Going for priesthood was not meant for boys who had qualified for secondary school. Anybody with a bare pass in the upper primary school-leaving examination could qualify for that. He would not throw away the opportunity to acquire higher education. If it was the Lord's design that he should serve him, it would be possible to do so after acquiring more education. That way, he could serve God better. The Lord deserved the best.

'Mama, it is a great idea to serve the Lord. But this is not the right time. I want to go to Chizongwe. It is the best secondary school in the province,' Isaki pleaded.

'Where will the fees come from? Education does not end. Leave it for those who have fathers.'

Isaki did not want to argue with his mother. He would give her time to reflect on what he had told her. Perhaps later she would understand his point of view. For now, he would have to put that issue on hold. He would come back to the matter when his acceptance letter arrived from Chizongwe.

The acceptance letter arrived a week later. It was a thick khaki envelope labelled ON HER MAJESTY'S SERVICE. Isaki opened the letter with a mixture of excitement and worry. He was excited to receive a letter which had come all the way from Fort Jameson on her majesty's service. But he was also worried because he did not know what kind of fees they were asking for.

The envelope contained quite a few sheets of paper. With trembling fingers, he sorted them out. The first was a letter informing him that he had been selected for Form One. He put that aside. He would read it later. The next was a set of school rules. He put that aside too. Then he picked up one that contained a list of requirements. That was the one he needed to study right away. His heart missed a beat. The fees were nineteen pounds and fifteen shillings. His mother could not raise that.

There was also a list of things that every boy was supposed to purchase in advance. He read through this list: two brand new pairs of black shoes, seven pairs of grey socks, seven handkerchiefs, seven underpants, seven vests, four bath towels, two face towels, a toothbrush, a tube of toothpaste, a black shoe brush, a tin of black shoe polish, a comb, a fountain pen and a bottle of blue or black ink.

He breathed a sigh of despair. Where would he find the money for all those things? He decided not to tell his mother the contents of the letter yet. He would think of ways of raising the money before he could talk to her. He resolved to write to his father and ask him for the fees. Perhaps he might send him the money now that he had qualified for secondary school.

He prayed for the response to his letter to arrive before the second week of July, for all those who had been selected for Form One were required to report on the second Monday of that month. It was only three days before he was due to report at Chizongwe that a letter arrived from his father.

23-6-61

My dear Isaki,

How are you? We are all well. You now have two young sisters here. The elder is three years old and the younger six months.

I was glad to learn that you have completed Standard Six. You also said you would like to go on to do Standard Seven. It is not wise to do so. Here, you can get a good job with a Standard Six certificate. The teachers at the farm school, for example, are only Standard Fours.

Come here and become a teacher. I can tell V.V. about you. He will be glad to have you. It will not take long before you become the head-teacher. If you like this idea, answer this letter quickly and I will send you transport money.

Greet everybody there.

I am your father of all times,

Musandivute.

Isaki wondered what advantages there would be in accepting a teaching job at a farm school. All he wanted was to go to secondary school. If he wanted to be a teacher, he would go to a teacher-training college. He would not go into a school that did not require him to go through formal training. Besides, what guarantee was there that V.V.'s farm school would always be there? He decided to discuss the matter with his mother again.

'I have been thinking about my education,' he began. 'As I said when I arrived home from Angoni, I want to go to secondary school. I know you would like me to train as a priest but I feel that will not be good for me. I want to be a doctor. '

'Does that not take too long?'

'It does, Mama. But once I get there, all will be fine. I believe that is what the Lord has in store for me. But of course, there are two problems. You already know about one – the fees. They want nineteen pounds and fifteen shillings.'

'That is impossible! Will anybody find that much money?'

'Some people will. Many parents do their best to raise the fees because Chizongwe is an excellent school. It is a pity my father does not take education seriously.'

'Your father does not take anything seriously. I am sorry to tell you this. If you wrote to him, he would not answer you. Whatever you plan to do, do not rely on him.'

'I have already written to him. He does not want me to go to secondary school. He has other plans for me. He says since I have completed Standard Six, I should go to Southern Rhodesia and become a teacher at the farm school.'

'What? I will not allow my child to be used like that! If you go there, he will let you rot at that tobacco school of theirs. That is where his wife teaches. Do you want to work side by side with her?'

'No! I do not want to be a teacher. Even if I did, I would not want to work at a farm school. All I want is to go to Chizongwe Secondary School for Form One.'

Tisa thought about her husband's suggestion. It was one of his tricks. His proposal was all for his own good. When Isaki needed school fees, he did not send him any. But now that he had completed Standard Six after a struggle, Musa wanted to take him away from his mother. He was becoming interested in Isaki only because he knew he would no longer be requiring any assistance. Tisa was not going to let her husband take her child away.

'No, my child, you must not agree. It is true that the secondary school fees are too much for us. But going to work at a farm school is not the solution. Stay here and we will see what we can do. If your father wants you to join him, let him come and collect you.'

Lying in bed that evening, Isaki considered his position and before he fell asleep, he made a number of resolutions. Firstly, he ruled out becoming an untrained farm school teacher. Secondly, he decided that priesthood was not his calling. Thirdly, he made up his mind that he would go to Chizongwe Secondary School, with or without fees. Lastly, he was going to write to his father and speak his mind.

Isaki left the village at dawn. He was required to report at Chizongwe the following day. He was going to walk there. Nkhanza was twenty-five miles away from Fort Jameson. The bus fare from Katawa to Fort Jameson was five shillings. He did not have any money. If he asked his mother, she would probably borrow and give it to him. But he did not want to bother her about his school business any longer. He did not even want her to know that he had decided to go to school. Isaki did not tell anybody but Yosefe about it because he wanted to fight his own battles.

He expected to cover the distance in two days. He would do fourteen miles on his first day and then take a rest. On the second day, he would cover the remaining eleven miles. Once in Fort Jameson, he would go to the bus station and wait there for a school truck from Chizongwe. According to the instructions in the letter of acceptance from the principal, a lorry would make two-hourly trips to and from the bus station on that day.

Although he had walked twenty-five miles to Fort Jameson, he did not want to be seen arriving at school on foot. On arrival in the town, he went to the bus station where he joined other boys. When they got to the school, all the Form One boys were told to gather under a big tree where they were instructed to wait for the principal. As he waited with his fellow Form One boys, Isaki was so exhausted that he decided to take a nap. He found a cool spot under a tree not far from the large tree where they were assembled and lay there. As usual, he did not have much baggage. All he had were his favourite two khaki paper bags. One contained six old uniforms from Angoni School whereas the other had some groundnuts and roasted sweet potatoes which he had taken from home the previous day.

Lying at a distance from his fellow Form One boys, Isaki rehearsed what he would tell the principal. He had been planning his strategy from the time he set out on his long walk to Chizongwe. This was not going to be the first time that he had come to school without fees. But in spite of his experience in handling such issues, he could not be complacent. He was aware that the two occasions were not similar. The situation at hand was more difficult than the previous one.

At Angoni, the fees were nine pounds and fifteen shillings whereas at Chizongwe they were double that amount. Secondly, whilst the headmaster of Angoni Upper Primary School was an ordinary African person from a typical African village, the principal of Chizongwe Secondary School was a white expatriate. He had heard some people say that the man was from England and others that he was a South African. But whether he was from England or from South Africa could not make any difference to his situation. The fact was that the fellow was not a black man. Isaki did not expect him to understand his problems.

But that did not make him give up. He had prayed a lot since the day that the headmaster of Angoni Upper School announced that he was one of the four boys who had been offered a place at Chizongwe. He had walked all the way from his village out of faith and he would soldier on out of faith until he faced the principal.

The principal was accompanied by two people. Isaki was pleased that the other two were black. He consoled himself with the thought that if the white principal found his story hard to believe, the two black fellows might understand and explain things to him in a language he would understand.

'Attention!' shouted one of the black men. 'The principal will explain a few things to you,' he told them and stepped back. The principal began to speak. To the surprise of the Form One boys, he had a small voice which did not sound authoritative.

'I welcome you all to Chizongwe Secondary School. As you know, our school takes only the best. The fact that we selected you means that you worked hard in primary school. Here, we'll expect you to work harder,' he told them and then paused.

'I want you to stand in a straight line. Keep your suitcase on your left. When we come to you, you must open it for us. We'll check the contents of your suitcase to ensure that you have brought all the items that were listed in your letter of acceptance. In case some of you do not remember what these items are, the boarding-master will read the list out to you.'

The black man who had spoken earlier stepped forward again and read the items one after the other, starting with two 'brand new pairs of black shoes'.

As the boarding-master read through the list, the boys touched each of the items named to make sure that they had not forgotten any of them. Isaki stood restlessly. He had no suitcase to open. Whilst his colleagues were busy looking at the items they had brought, he worried about where to place himself in the queue. He did not want to be in front for he needed to give himself time to rehearse what he was going to say to the principal. He did not want to be at the very rear either. So he stood somewhere in the centre. The centre position was good for it gave him the opportunity to observe how the principal dealt with those boys who lacked one thing or another.

'Show me your two brand new pairs of black shoes,' the principal would order each boy he came to. Where one pro-duced the required two pairs, he would ask for the next item on the list until he had checked all fourteen items. In the case of a boy who had only one pair of shoes or had two but not quite brand new ones, he would tell him to go back home and bring the required two brand new pairs. Isaki waited for his turn nervously and began to regret that he ever came. Although he had been thinking of what to say for a long time, now that the moment had come, he was not sure how to say it. As the principal closed in on him, Isaki moved two or three positions backwards. He prayed to God to give him courage, politeness and wisdom when his turn came.

Eventually, his turn arrived. The first thing the principal noticed was the absence of a suitcase on this boy's left-hand side. He turned to his right but saw no suitcase there either. Then he studied the boy from toes to head. He was confused. He did not know what to say to the boy. How could he ask him to show him two brand new pairs of black shoes when he could see that the boy did not have even an old pair on his feet? The principal stood speechless beside the boy. Noticing his state of shock, the boarding-master rushed to his rescue. He was not going to allow any of the new boys to embarrass the black race by demonstrating poverty in front of a white man – especially since that white man happened to be the principal of the best secondary school in the province. He stared angrily at the boy without a suitcase. When he did not show any signs of being moved by that stare, he screamed at him in Cinyanja.

'What brings you here? This is Chizongwe Secondary School. It is not some primary school. Go away!' he roared at him.

'Excuse me, sir,' began Isaki, 'I was accepted for Form One here. My name is Isaki Manda. Here is my acceptance letter,' he added, presenting the letter to him.

The principal grabbed the letter from the boy and went straight for his signature. Then he looked at him again – carefully this time. He gave Isaki his letter back and, without uttering a word, signalled to him to step aside. Isaki moved off the queue and the principal continued inspecting the rest of the boys' suitcases. When he had seen every boy, he told all those who had not brought the required items to go back to their parents who must buy them.

When that group had left, he addressed the remaining ones. Thereafter, he turned to the boarding-master and said, 'Tell that boy without a suitcase to come to my office. You come too.'

The boarding-master pulled Isaki by the arm. Isaki was no longer nervous. He had gathered enough courage. He did not think he should be afraid of anybody for he was not on trial. He had not stolen anything. He was not telling any lies either. He was merely a poor boy who needed to get some education. The Lord would help him. He remembered Mark chapter eleven, verse twenty-four: 'Therefore, I tell you, whatever you ask for in prayer, believe that you have received it, and it will be yours.'

The principal asked him a few questions.

'Which primary school are you from?'

'Angoni Upper School, sir.'

'What's your name?'

'Isaki Manda.'

The principal paused and began to consult a file in front of him. As he studied that file, he shook his head in a manner which gave the impression that he was particularly displeased about something.

'Where is your suitcase?' he resumed the questioning.

'I have no suitcase, sir.'

'Show me your two brand new pairs of black shoes.'

'I have no shoes, sir.'

'Well, show me your four bath towels, then.'

'Sir, I have not brought anything – not even the fees.'

'You did not bring anything?' asked the boarding-master.

'No, sir.'

'What did you think you were coming to? This is a boarding-school and not an orphanage,' the boarding master screamed.

Isaki bowed his head and prayed. The principal continued staring at him in sheer surprise.

'Do you have a father?' the principal asked.

'Yes, sir.'

'Where is he?'

'In Southern Rhodesia.'

'Does he know you have been offered a place at Chizongwe?'

'Yes, sir. I wrote to him when I got the acceptance letter.'

'And when did he say he would be sending the fees?'

'He did not promise to send any money, sir.'

'What? You told him you have a place at Chizongwe Secondary School and he did not promise to send you the fees?'

'He didn't, sir. He told me that I should go to Southern Rhodesia to become a teacher at a farm school.'

'And your mother? Is she also in Southern Rhodesia?'

'No, sir. She is in the village.'

'What did she say about the fees?'

'Nothing, sir. She wants me to train as a priest.'

'And yourself, what would you like to do?'

'Sir, I want to continue learning. That is why I walked the twenty-five miles from my village to come here even though I have no money.'

'Did you think you would be admitted without any money?' the boarding-master asked him. 'Why don't you go back and sell one cow? Doesn't your father have cattle in the village?'

'He does, but I can't sell any.'

'Why can't you?' the principal enquired.

'Because my young father won't let me, sir.'

'What do you mean by your young father?'

'He means his uncle, sir. His father's younger brother,' the boarding-master explained.

'So you have a guardian in the village? You must go back home and ask that young father of yours to give you the fees. If he can't find nineteen pounds and fifteen shillings now, he may give you seven pounds and five shillings which is the instalment for this school term. Meanwhile, we will keep your place for two weeks. If you don't come after two weeks, we'll offer the place to someone else.'

'Yes,' the boarding-master concurred. 'There are many boys on the waiting list who have nineteen pounds and fifteen shillings. Go and tell your young father to sell one bull quickly or you'll lose your place in this school.'

Isaki walked out of the principal's office reluctantly. He did not think going back to the village would help him. Baba Shuzi would never allow him to sell any cattle. To make matters worse, Baba Shuzi did not believe in children being in school. Isaki would have to think of other means of raising the fees without having to return to the village.

For that night, however, he needed somewhere to sleep. At the bus station in Fort Jameson, there were often people who spent nights there whilst waiting for the next bus to their destination. He would join those people for the night. Nobody would suspect that he was not destined for any place.

He arrived at the bus station after sunset. There were many people, some queuing for tickets, others walking about aimlessly and others lying all over the place. Isaki was not going to pretend to be waiting for a bus. He would look for a free corner where he could catch some rest. But every corner was occupied either by people or by piles of suitcases. Feeling tired, he squeezed himself between the suitcases. While he sat there squashed between the suitcases, a man who had been standing in the queue for tickets accosted him.

'Hey, what are you doing there? Those are not your cases.'

'No, baba.'

'Why are you sitting so close to them, then?'

'Forgive me, baba,' Isaki apologised. 'I'm tired. I only want to rest.'

'Boy, you can't cheat me. You're a pickpocket.'

'Please, baba, believe me. I'm not a pickpocket.'

'That's what you all say. During the day, you sleep but at night you come here to steal from innocent travellers. You were not here during the day, were you? Tell me the truth. I know the people who have been struggling for buses here since morning. You weren't here, were you?'

'No, baba. You're right I wasn't here.'

'You see now. And where could you have come from at this time? I did not see any bus arrive. Have you come from some home within town?'

'No, baba.'

'You see! You haven't come from anywhere. You're one of those homeless boys who come to Fort Jameson to steal from travellers. Why don't you stay in your village and look after your father's cattle?'

Isaki did not answer. He bowed his head and said a short prayer.

'What are you looking down for?' the man asked. 'Didn't you hear what I said?'

'I did, baba.'

'So? Why don't you answer me? Boys of your age should be in school instead of loitering around town. If you're too dull to be in school, it is better for you to stay in the village and look after cattle.'

'Yes, baba. I should be in school. But I have no school fees. I was at Chizongwe where I reported for Form One but the principal sent me away because I have no money.'

The man was now speechless. The boy did not look like

someone who had a place in Form One, let alone at Chizongwe.

'My boy, stand up,' he asked him. 'I would like to have a good look at you,' he added in English. And Isaki obliged. The man then eyed him from his bare feet to head.

'You were selected for Form One at Chizongwe?'

'Yes, sir,' said Isaki and, reading some doubt on the man's face, he dipped his hand into one of his paper bags. He drew out a khaki envelope labelled ON HER MAJESTY'S SERVICE which he gave to the man, saying, 'Here's my acceptance letter, sir.'

The man took the letter, walked to a spot where he could find some light and began to read. Halfway through the letter, he folded it, put it into its envelope and gave it back to the owner. Thereafter, he studied the boy all over again.

'So you have a place at one of the best secondary schools in the country and you're not taking it up! I can't believe it. Do you know how many boys right now wish they had been accepted at that school?' the man asked.

Isaki did not say anything.

'Where are you going, now?' asked the man.

'Nowhere.'

'Nowhere? What are you at the bus station for, then?'

'I need somewhere to sleep.'

'And tomorrow? What will you do?'

'I don't know. Maybe I'll go back to Chizongwe and plead with the principal to allow me to start school while I look for money. Maybe I'll walk back home and discuss with my mother what to do next.'

'Don't you have a father?'

'I do, but he is in Southern Rhodesia.'

'Why didn't you write to him to send you the fees?'

'He doesn't want me to continue with school. He says I should go there and start teaching at a farm school. But I don't want that.'

Then neither of them spoke for some time.

'I'm sorry for having taken you for a pickpocket, my boy,' the man told Isaki. 'You're a bright boy who is unfortunate enough to have a father who doesn't understand the value of education.

I only went up to Standard Six myself. But that wasn't because of lack of fees. I didn't get a Form One place anywhere.'

'What do you do now?' asked Isaki.

'Well, I'm a postal clerk in Kitwe. I'm going back there now. I was home on a short leave. Tell me something, boy. You said you may have to walk home tomorrow?'

'Yes.'

'How far is your home?'

'Twenty-five miles.'

'And you want to walk all that distance?'

'Yes. That is how I came. I have no bus fare.'

'How much is the fare?'

'Five shillings.'

'I'll give you the five shillings,' the man offered. 'In the meantime, whilst I queue for my ticket, could you stay right where you are and look after my suitcase?'

Isaki found company in the man that night.

THIRTEEN

Tisa was pleased to see her son safely back home. When he narrated all that transpired at Chizongwe Secondary School, they agreed to ask Shuzi to sell one bull for the boarding fees.

'Mama, what has befallen us this evening?' asked Shuzi when they called on him.

'It is about Isaki, baba. He has been sent back from school to fetch fees,' said Tisa. 'He will explain the rest alone.'

Isaki told Shuzi the whole story.

'Mother of Isaki,' Shuzi began, 'is this how to live? The two of you decided that the boy should go to school. You did not consult me. You wanted to show the whole world that you could do without me. Now that he has been sent back home, you bring him to me. Am I a fool to be told by a woman what to do? Since you did not ask me in the first instance, do not bother me this time. You started it alone and so, conclude it on your own.'

'But baba, it is your child. When he left the village, I was not aware. Isaki, tell your father.'

'Baba, I am sorry that I did not tell you when I left home. I did not tell my mother either. I only told Yosefe. I did not tell anyone because I did not want to bother anyone. Secondly, I knew that if I told you or my mother, you would not let me go. But now that I have been sent back, I feel that I should discuss the matter with you. I know that nineteen pounds and fifteen shillings is a lot of money. But I came because I thought we could sell one or two bulls. If we sold two, I could pay the amount at once.'

Shuzi laughed and his senior wife, Nyanya, joined him.

'Mother of Isaki, is that what you have been telling my child?' Shuzi asked and relapsed into laughter. 'What can we expect from a male child who spends all his time listening to his mother? Ours is not what any real Ngoni man can call a kraal. Is it wise of any boy to think of selling even a single animal from such a small kraal?' he asked, and paused.

'Isaki,' he continued, 'never listen to women. Those cattle are for you and your brothers and your sons. Do not sell any. The wealth of a Ngoni man lies in his cattle. I must tell you this, for I am the only one who can. I do not want people to accuse me when I am dead of having concealed the truth from you.'

And then, silence fell upon them.

'Mother of Isaki, those are my only words,' said Shuzi.

'We have heard your words, baba,' said Tisa. 'May you sleep well,' she added. She tapped her son on the shoulder as she rose to leave. Isaki followed her.

'What shall we do?' Isaki asked his mother.

'I do not know,' she told him.

'Why don't I sell one bull without his consent?'

'Nobody would risk buying a cow from a boy, my child.'

'What if you accompanied me and vouched for me?' he asked, and Tisa laughed.

'Why do you laugh at me like my young father did?'

'Because what you said is ridiculous. Do you think anyone could buy a cow from a woman? A woman is not expected to have any say in these matters. She is not expected to have any say even in connection with those cattle that were paid to her father as cimalo by her husband.'

'That is not fair. You mean you have no say over the cattle which my father gave my grandfather for your marriage?'

'I don't, my child.'

'If you asked him to sell one for my fees, would he refuse?'

'Go and ask him. He is your grandfather.'

Isaki wondered why he had not thought of that. Perhaps his grandfather was the answer. He could sell one or two bulls from his kraal and pay his full boarding-fees.

Before sunrise the following morning, Isaki set off for Mtendere all alone. He did not want his mother to accompany him lest she be accused again by Shuzi of poisoning his mind.

'Is it well where you have come from?' Lwando asked.

'All is well, baba.'

'Is your mother well?' his grandmother enquired.

'She is well.'

'What brings you here, then?' his grandfather asked.

'Why do you ask him such a question? Don't you expect him to visit his grandparents?' Mwaziona complained.

'Mwaziona, Isaki must grow up. Don't expect him to remain your baby grandson for ever. He should be helping his mother fell trees for a new field before the rains come. Moreover, since his father is in Walale, this boy should be doing for his mother what his father would have been doing if he were at home.'

'Were you felling trees in your mother's fields when you were his age?'

'What are you talking about? At his age, I had my own fields and was filling up my parents' granary.'

'Grandmother, I can defend myself. Do not worry about what your husband says about me. He feels jealous now that your younger and stronger husband is here.'

'Stronger husband? If you were strong, you would not be walking around so lazily. If you are a real man, let us hear your explanation for your wasting valuable time like this,' Lwando challenged him.

Briefly, Isaki explained his problem again.

'I thought there was no reason why I should continue to suffer as if my mother were not born of reputable people. So, I came to ask you to sell one or two of your cattle so that I may obtain the fees and return to school. Please, help me. There is nobody else I can turn to,' Isaki concluded.

'Baba, are those not words?' Mwaziona asked. 'How many boys of nowadays think the way your grandson does? One day, he will look after your daughter whose husband has abandoned her.'

Lwando remained quiet for some time. He did not know how he would make the boy understand. He had cattle and selling two for his fees would not leave a big hole in his kraal. But paying fees for his son-in-law's son would be improper. That would be like returning his cimalo and malowolo.

'Isaki, it is wise of you to recognise that your mother was born of reputable parents.'

'You will help me then?' Isaki interrupted his grandfather.

'Hold your mouth. That is one problem with you boys born in

Walale. The selling of cattle is such a serious matter that it cannot be decided by one head. We are not talking about goats or chickens. I wish I could tell you that I will give you the cattle, but I cannot. What would people say about me? I am not going to treat you as if you were an illegitimate child. You have a father. It would be wrong of me to give you cattle without asking him.'

'So, you will not give me the cattle?'

'Wait till I finish. You must write to your father and ask for his consent. Once he says it is alright, I will not only give you two bulls but will let you choose them for yourself.'

'Oh no! That will not help me.'

'Why not?'

'I was given only two weeks in which to find the fees. If I am not back at Chizongwe within two weeks, my place will be given away. If you will let me have the bulls only after I get a letter from my father, it will be too late. Besides, my father will not allow me to get the animals from you for he does not want me to continue with school. When I wrote to him, he told me that I must stop school and become a teacher at V.V.'s farm school. I do not want to do that.'

'That is what I feared. My child, if you want to be successful in life, never do things against your father's wishes. He may be far away, but he is still your father. My advice is that if you think writing to him would be too late, you should ask Baba Shuzi to talk to me about it.'

Isaki returned to Nkhanza bitter with Shuzi for refusing to sell his father's cattle. He wondered if Shuzi cared at all about what sort of future he and his brothers had. All Shuzi wanted out of them was free labour. He would make Isaki's brothers look after cattle till they were too old to go to school. That kraal was jointly owned by Isaki's father and Shuzi, but the cattle were as good as Shuzi's alone for he had complete control over what happened to them. Isaki's father was never consulted.

Back in Nkhanza, Isaki briefed his mother about what his grandfather had told him. Thereafter, he told her that he had decided to tell Yosefe to stop looking after cattle, for doing so was worthless.

'My child,' Tisa pleaded, 'do not do that. You will only create more problems for me.'

'Do not worry, mother. We will do it in such a way that he will know you have had no part in it.'

When he discussed the plan with Yosefe, Isaki learnt something which he did not know before. Yosefe said he could predict how Shuzi would react.

'He will instruct our mother not to give me any food until I go back to look after cattle. That will hurt our mother.'

'Don't worry,' said Isaki. 'Tomorrow morning, we must leave for Mtendere. There, we should tell our grandparents that we're merely visiting. They won't chase us away. We'll be there long enough for Baba Shuzi to feel your absence.'

'But eventually we'll come back home and he'll punish us. Why don't we accept the fact that we have to suffer because our father abandoned us?'

Isaki considered Yosefe's words. Did they have to suffer just because their father had forsaken them?

'Do we have to come back?' Isaki asked. 'What would happen if we didn't return? Our grandparents would not force us to leave. Even if they did tell us to leave, what would they do if we refused to?'

'I don't know.'

'Nothing. No grandparents would chase their grandchildren away. Tomorrow, let's leave this village.'

'Shall we leave our mother alone?'

'She will be alright. If we sit idle, her situation will never change. If anything, her problems will worsen. Let's try this plan. It might help her.'

When Shuzi learnt that Yosefe had not gone to look after cattle, he trembled with fury. If he were ill, his mother would have informed him. He was not going to tolerate laziness. Firstly, he would flog him. Thereafter, he would instruct Yosefe's mother not to feed him for two days. He stood outside his house and called out the boy's name. When he got no response, he called out Isaki's name. There was no answer from him either.

'Where are these boys?' he asked.

Tisa approached him and, at a little distance, she knelt down and greeted him.

'I heard you call your children's names, baba. I am also worried for I have not seen them. What do the other boys say?'

'Nothing. Are you not hiding them?' asked Shuzi.

'Baba, why would I do such a thing?'

'How can I trust you, mother of Isaki? This is not the first time that you and your child have done something behind my back.'

'When did I ever do anything behind your back? Whenever Isaki has asked me something, have I not always brought him before you?'

'You want to deny it? Mother of Isaki, admit it and we will not be here all night long. Do you want me to narrate to you all that you have done since my brother left you in this village? Was it not you who decided that Isaki should start school? You had him signed up for Sairi. That was the beginning of my problems.

'A year later, you moved him to a boarding-school at Angoni. The school sent him back home because he did not have fees. But you did not give up. You used some kind of influence and a teacher followed the boy all the way here. Again, you agreed with the teacher that Isaki should return to school. Up to this day, only you know where the fees came from for the four years that he was at Angoni School.

'Then, only this week, the boy left the village for Fort Jameson to join a secondary school. Did you tell me about that? And now, both Isaki and Yosefe are missing. Once again, only you know where they are. I know you will tell me only when it suits you. Is that how I am going to live with you?'

Tisa did not say anything.

'Tell me where you are hiding them?' continued Shuzi.

'I do not know where they are.'

'If that is true, let us agree on two things. As soon as they come home, tell me. Secondly, you must not give them any food until I say so.'

Tisa remained silent.

'Those are my words,' concluded Shuzi. And without any

further word, he turned away from her and walked into his house.

Tisa rose from her kneeling position and left. Once alone, she went into a sulk over what Shuzi had said. Why had he accused her of crimes she had not committed? She decided to complain to the headman.

The headman's advice was to wait until the following morning. If the boys did not show up by then, it would be necessary to start looking for them in every likely place. As for the harsh words from her brother-in-law, headman Nkhanza told her that it was nothing to be depressed about.

'In the morning, if the boys are still at large, come here again and we will decide what to do.'

Tisa followed the headman's advice reluctantly. Her sons would not have left home for no reason. Shuzi had driven them away. The following day, she would start looking for them. Early in the morning, she would call on the headman again and tell him her plans. She had decided to go to Mtendere.

Lwando and Mwaziona received their grandsons with mixed feelings. While they were happy to see them, they were suspicious of the reason for their visit. Isaki had been with them only the other day. If they were now merely visiting, why didn't he tell them about it then?

'Your grandchildren must have run away from home,' Lwando told his wife.

'I agree with you, baba. What shall we do when they do not want to tell us the truth?'

'Let us give them some time. By the end of tomorrow, they should tell us why they are here.'

'And if they do not?'

'I think they will. If they continue being silent, we will have to think of ways of extracting the truth out of them.'

Headman Nkhanza did not like Tisa's decision to look for her children on her own. He advised Shuzi to accompany her.

'Why should I go with her?' asked Shuzi. 'Mother of Isaki

created this problem and so she must sort it out alone. If she had not been handling these boys as if they were illegitimate children, they would not have thought of fleeing from home. We paid malowolo for these children. That they ran away to their mother's village is despicable.'

'I agree that the boys' action has brought our village into disrepute. But if we let their mother follow them on her own, we will bring greater shame unto ourselves. What will the men of Mtendere think of us?'

As headman Nkhanza talked to Shuzi, Tisa set off. She could not wait. In the meantime, in Mtendere, Lwando waited until his grandchildren had taken their mid-morning meal before interviewing them.

'Now, my boys,' he began, 'how did you pass the night?'

'Very well,' answered Isaki.

Lwando deliberately allowed some silence to reign for a while. Yosefe began to fear that their grandfather might whip them for having run away from their home. He wished he had not agreed to come with his brother. He looked at his grandfather's face and then at his grandmother's. Neither of them showed any signs of anger. That surprised him.

'I called you boys because I want to discuss something with you. Do not be afraid. Remember that as your grandfather, I am your best friend in the whole world,' he assured them and smiled. Their grandmother also smiled. Yosefe relaxed.

'We are happy to see you,' he continued. 'However, we are saddened because you look unhappy. We want you to know that you were right to come. Whenever anything bothers you, remember that we are always prepared to listen to you. There must be no secrets between you and us. Now, tell us what is worrying you.'

'You are right,' Isaki began. 'We are not happy. Yosefe and I are fed up with living like orphans. I need money for fees. Our father is in Southern Rhodesia where he has a good job but he has refused to send us any money. In the meantime, Yosefe spends days and days in the forest on an empty stomach looking after Baba Shuzi's cattle. This man is a father only when he needs our labour. Whenever we ask for help, he refuses. He has refused to sell any of our father's bulls to raise my fees. We are fed up with him. That is why we came.'

'And what do you want us to do?'

'Nothing. We will just be with you from now onwards.'

'For ever?'

'Until our father comes to fetch us. Yosefe can start looking after your cattle.'

'Those are words, baba,' said Mwaziona. 'What have I always told you? Tisa has wise children. They will look after your daughter in her old age.'

Lwando considered his grandchild's words. Isaki had spoken the truth. His father had abandoned them. But what could Lwando tell him at that stage? He would wait for a delegation from Nkhanza. If that village had men, they would follow the boys.

'Does Baba Shuzi know that you are here?' Lwando asked.

'I do not know,' said Isaki. 'We did not tell anybody that we were coming here.'

'Boys, I hear your words. But there is nothing I can do now. I will wait until I hear from Baba Shuzi.'

Late that afternoon, they saw someone arrive. To their disappointment, it was not their son-in-law. Nor was it his representative. It was their daughter, Tisa.

'Mother of Isaki!' exclaimed Lwando. 'It is not you that I have been expecting.'

'Who have you been expecting, baba?'

'You know why your children are here?'

'I don't, baba. But I thought they may be. That is why I followed them,' said Tisa.

Lwando explained to her all that Isaki had told them.

'Does Baba Shuzi know that his children are here?' Lwando asked.

'He knows that they are not in Nkhanza. He enquired about them the day they left. He wanted to flog them. He also instructed me not to feed them for two days upon their return.'

'So, why is he not looking for them? That is what any caring father is expected to do,' said Lwando.

'I do not know, baba. I do not understand my brother-in-law. I do not think he likes us. We are a burden to him. His brother does not care about us either. Why should he bother?'

'My child,' Mwaziona began, 'something is wrong with father of Isaki. I believe he is the one to blame for all your troubles. It is all because he married that woman out there in Walale. I wonder why you should still be married to him.'

'There you go with your long lips again. Those are not words,' Lwando complained. 'We should be building and not destroying. Our son-in-law has children with our daughter. Being a grandmother of these children, your duty should be ensuring that their parents' marriage survives.'

A short moment of silence followed.

'Mother of Isaki,' resumed Lwando, 'you must not have such thoughts. I know that the people of Nkhanza are not giving you the respect befitting a woman who has borne them so many children. But do not despair. If you keep the dignity that your husband found you with when he married you, then one day, he will come back to you, pleading.'

'Father of Isaki is conceited,' said Mwaziona. 'He will never plead. Tisa must ask for a divorce.'

Lwando clapped his hands once and then capped his mouth with the left hand. He was speechless. Tisa noticed her father's reaction and intervened.

'Baba,' she began, 'you are right that I must strive to retain my dignity. I will do that. I do not mind what those people in Nkhanza say about me. The only thing that saddens me is making my children suffer as well. No matter what they do to me, I will be in that village until father of Isaki decides to divorce me. I will never contemplate divorcing him.'

'Why not?' asked Mwaziona. 'Why should you continue to be abused like that as if you were not born of people? My child, you have a perfect home here in Mtendere.'

'Mother, I am a Christian. I cannot divorce my husband. If he does not want this marriage, it is he who must initiate divorce proceedings.'

'My child, does the Bible say that you must not divorce even when your husband has abandoned you?' asked Mwaziona.

'Mother,' said Tisa, 'here is what the Bible says about marriage and divorce. I will read from one Corinthians chapter seven, verses ten and eleven.'

> To the married I give this command (not I, but
> the Lord): A wife must not separate from her husband.
> But if she does, she must remain unmarried
> or else be reconciled to her husband. And a husband
> must not divorce his wife.

'Thank you for that scripture, mother of Isaki,' said Lwando. 'Please, remain strong in your faith for it will save you from wasting away with anger. As you correctly put it, we should worry about what happens to the children. What do you suggest that we do about Isaki and Yosefe?'

'I do not know, baba. It is up to you. I am sure Isaki has told you what his plans are.'

'He has. But I am afraid we cannot go by the plans of a boy, especially of a boy who is angry. What he has in mind is that he and his young brother will remain here until his father comes from Walale to fetch them. Now, when will that be?

'I suggest that you return to Nkhanza with a message from me to Baba Shuzi. Tell him that his children are here and that they came with a complaint which we would like to discuss with him. In the meantime, the two boys will be here till he comes. I am suggesting this in order to reach a compromise with Isaki. His wish is that his father should come all the way from Walale to Mtendere. Since his father cannot come soon, we had better advise him to accept this compromise. What do you think?'

'Those are words, baba. I am glad that I found my children here. How long they stay does not matter to me. At least I know they are in good hands. I will pass on your message to Baba Shuzi in the presence of headman Nkhanza,' said Tisa.

Isaki began to worry about his schooling again. It was over a week since he was sent back home from Chizongwe Secondary School. He was not going to wait for Shuzi in Mtendere indefinitely. He would go back to school and face the principal.

One of his immediate problems was how to convince his grandparents of the necessity for him to leave for Fort Jameson. If he told them of his plans, they might stop him. The best approach would be to take off without saying farewell. It would hurt them, but some day, he would be back to explain his actions.

His other problem was in connection with Yosefe. Was he going to leave him alone with the grandparents? He would die of boredom. One alternative could be to take him back to Nkhanza first, before proceeding to Chizongwe himself. But that would be unfair to his young brother for Shuzi would vent all his anger on him.

Another option would be to find something for him to do whilst waiting for Shuzi to come to Mtendere. He could start looking after their grandfather's cattle. Or he could start school. Isaki felt attracted to the latter idea.

Sairi Lower Primary School was within walking distance from Mtendere. And maybe the headmaster of four years ago was still there. If he was, getting a place for Yosefe would not be a problem. That headmaster would remember Isaki as having been the best pupil during his year. He would take Yosefe there.

Isaki foresaw only one hurdle in the execution of his plan. The headmaster of Sairi might insist on seeing their parent or guardian before enrolling Yosefe. How would Isaki make his grandfather act as the guardian? He should have thought of it whilst their mother was around. She would not have refused to give her consent. He decided to ask their grandmother to stand in for their mother.

Their grandmother agreed to help. She was going to persuade her husband to put Yosefe in school. Once that was done, anyone wishing to remove him from the school would have to battle it out with the headmaster. Both Isaki and his grandmother knew that the headmaster of Sairi did not take kindly to parents who refused to have their children enrolled in school, let alone to those who attempted to withdraw their children from there.

Persuading Lwando turned out to be easy. After a heated

discussion, Mwaziona offered her husband a compromise. She would stop pushing Tisa for a divorce if he promised to co-operate with their grandsons.

Lwando considered the matter from several angles and finally agreed with his wife.

'That will sort Yosefe out,' remarked Lwando after they had agreed to take the boy to school. 'But we still have Isaki's problem. What shall we do about him? He needs nineteen pounds and fifteen shillings to proceed with school.'

'Isaki knows how to persevere,' said Mwaziona. 'If we assure him that Yosefe is in safe hands, he will look after himself. That is what suffering has taught him.'

The following morning, Lwando asked Isaki what plans he had made for himself.

'I am going back to Chizongwe,' he announced.

'But you have no fees,' said his grandfather.

'Do not worry about that. I go by faith. That is one good thing my mother has taught me. All I have to do is ask and the Lord will provide. I did it before and God provided me with the fees for four years. That was how I completed my primary school. I believe that the Lord will provide again. All I ask is that you look after Yosefe now and ensure that he goes to school.'

Lwando patiently listened to his grandson and wondered why his son-in-law had abandoned a boy who thought like a grown-up at such an age.

FOURTEEN

Isaki spent the night at the bus station again, and walked to Chizongwe the following morning. Outside the principal's office, a long queue had formed. From the suitcases piled up outside the office, Isaki guessed that the boys in the queue were those who had not initially qualified for a place. Such boys brought the full school fees. That made him despair. How could the principal resist the cash from all those boys? Because of their presence, his bargaining power would be greatly reduced.

When Isaki's turn came, his knees trembled with a mixture of anxiety and despair. His feet nearly refused to move. But he dragged himself forward. As he walked into the office, he wished he would find the principal in a busy state for that would allow him more time to sharpen the strategy he had planned.

But the principal was all too ready for Isaki. As he entered the office, the man was already looking him straight in the eyes. And when Isaki stood at attention, the principal gave him the impression that he was just the boy he had been waiting for the whole morning.

'Good morning, sir,' Isaki greeted the principal.

'Good morning,' he replied.

'I'm back, sir,' said Isaki. 'I was here two weeks ago when school opened, sir. You sent me home because I had no fees.'

'Oh, I see,' said the principal as he picked up a file labelled SCHOOL FEES.

'What's your name?'

'Isaki Manda, sir.'

The principal started to peruse the file.

'My dear boy, how much money have you brought?'

'I haven't brought any, sir,' said Isaki.

This was the question he had been expecting. The principal looked up and began to study the boy in front of him from head to foot. He recalled the day two weeks before when this same boy had arrived at school not only without fees but without any suitcase.

'Do you believe that any secondary school will take a boy like you?'

Isaki did not answer.

'Get out of my office and go back home. I don't like boys who waste my time.'

Isaki did not move. He stood at attention. The principal let him stand for a short while.

'Didn't you hear what I said?' he roared at him. Isaki hesitantly turned away and started to walk out of the office.

'Next!' the principal called.

Outside, Isaki began to think. Where would he go and for what purpose? If he went back to Nkhanza, he would face the wrath of Shuzi. And if he returned to his grandparents in Mtendere, they would tell him to wait there until Shuzi came to fetch him. He would not go back to either village. Something else must be done. Someone somewhere might understand his position. The principal would listen to him if he persevered. He was going to wait outside the office until the principal had seen everyone. Thereafter, Isaki would knock at his door and get in. He was going to plead with him. If he went away, the principal would give his place to one of the boys who were queuing outside his office.

And so Isaki waited. He was there when the principal walked out at ten in the morning to drive to his house for tea. He was there when the principal returned to his office thirty minutes later. He was there when the principal and everybody else went away for lunch at twelve-thirty. And he was there when the principal came back for the afternoon session at two.

All this time, Isaki had hoped that the principal would ask him why he was still around. But the principal did not say anything. In fact, he behaved as if he had never seen him before. Isaki had hoped that someone would ask him whether or not he had eaten anything since morning. But nobody did.

By three that afternoon, he had a splitting headache. His lips were dry and beginning to show signs of cracking. His tummy was empty and rumbling. His knees were wobbly. And his eyes were watering and turning red. Outside the principal's office, he was the only boy left. He decided to pluck up some courage and knock at the door.

'Come in!' the principal responded.

Isaki staggered in and did his best to stand at some sort of attention. But that was all he could manage. As he stood there in front of the man he had seen hours earlier, Isaki did not have the energy to open his dry mouth. And even if he did, he was not sure how to start. So he stood there and looked straight into the principal's face.

'Yes, Isaki?' began the principal. And he liked it. At least, he remembered his name. 'You're still here?' the principal continued.

'Yes, sir.'

'But I told you to go away.'

'Yes, sir.'

'Why are you still here, then?'

'Sir, please give me a chance. I want to learn. Please!'

The principal studied the boy again. He had sent boys away before for lack of fees. But this one was different. The boys who reported without fees in the past at least had clothes. They had shoes. And they had suitcases. But this boy had nothing. Something else: this boy was persistent. He seemed to know what he wanted. There must be something inside him that made him so tenacious. Perhaps by admitting this boy and giving him a chance to raise his fees, he would be making a huge contribution to the history of the school and eventually to that of the country. This boy could be one of the great future leaders.

'Did you have any lunch?'

'No, sir.'

'Did you have any breakfast?'

'No, sir.'

The principal stopped there. He had no further questions.

'Wait outside,' he ordered him. Thereafter, he called the boarding-master on the phone.

As he waited outside the principal's office, Isaki prayed, thanking the Lord for what was beginning to happen to him.

Walking past him on his way to the headmaster's office, the boarding-master stopped and stared at him. After eyeing him from his bare toes to his head, he frowned at him.

'Aren't you the chap we sent away a fortnight ago?' the boarding-master quizzed him.

'I am, sir.'

'So, why are you here again?'

'Sir, I want to go to school. Please, help me.'

The boarding-master sighed and proceeded to knock at the principal's office. He was there for quite a while. In the meantime, feeling exhausted and hungry, Isaki decided to sit in a corner at a distance directly opposite the principal's office. From that corner, he continued to pray. He thanked God for what was happening and asked the Lord to fill the heart of the principal with boundless kindness. And then he dozed off.

He was asleep when he felt someone touch him. Opening his eyes with a start, the face in front of him slowly materialised into that of the boarding-master. Saliva was slowly oozing out of Isaki's mouth and his eyes were red. His tummy continued to rumble with emptiness.

'Come with me,' said the boarding-master in a tone which was surprisingly considerate and soft.

Isaki's knees felt much wobblier than they had done before he fell asleep. Walking behind the boarding-master was a struggle as his head ached terribly. Following blindly, he wondered what the two men had decided.

They came to his office. The boarding-master unlocked the door and went in. Isaki remained outside. He remembered what he had been taught in primary school. He had been told never to enter a teacher's house or office without knocking thrice on the door.

'Come in,' the boarding-master invited him as he was about to knock. Once inside, Isaki froze to attention in typical military style exactly as he had been taught in primary school.

'My boy,' the boarding-master began, 'we believe you deserve a place here because of your good Standard Six results as well as your determination to continue with your education. In the meantime, we'll start looking for a bursary for you.'

'Thank you very much, sir.'

'I'll now give you two uniforms, two blankets and one white cotton blanket. Work hard and follow the school rules,' the boarding-master told him and then dismissed him.

FIFTEEN

Yosefe was eleven years old when he went to Sairi Lower Primary School. The boy wanted to start from Sub B. The headmaster resisted, arguing that there was no basis for promoting a boy who had just been enrolled.

'Please sir, try me in Sub B because I did both Sub A and Sub B in Southern Rhodesia five years ago,' pleaded Yosefe.

'Five years ago? That is more reason why I should not promote you to Sub B. You surely have forgotten what you learnt there.'

'I haven't, sir. I have been reading my elder brother's books. My elder brother, Isaki, was here for one year. He did only Standard Two and went on to Angoni Upper School where he recently completed Standard Six.'

'Isaki? He's one of the best boys I have ever had at Sairi. Where's he now?' the headmaster asked.

'He has just gone to Chizongwe Secondary School, sir.'

'I'm not surprised. Your elder brother is bright,' said the headmaster. Turning to Lwando, he said, 'That grandson of yours, baba, is brilliant. Maybe all your grandchildren are brilliant. I'll try this one in Sub B as he suggests.'

Yosefe smiled. He was to start school the following day.

Back in Nkhanza, Tisa went to see the headman.

'How was your journey?' asked headman Nkhanza.

'Very well, baba. I am glad to let you know that I found your sons there and left them in good health. I am here to inform you that I have a message for my brother-in-law from my father. I felt that I should convey this message to Baba Shuzi in your presence because it is a serious matter,' she told the headman.

'What is the message, mama?'

'It is about the boys. They went to my father with a complaint about their young father. My father says that he will not release them until he has discussed their complaint with Baba Shuzi.'

'Mama, I hear the message. I will call Shuzi here tonight. When he is here, I will send for you. But let me point out that your husband paid malowolo in full for his children. For that reason, our father-in-law has no right to detain them. The boys do not belong there. They are ours.'

That evening, headman Nkhanza briefed Shuzi and the nduna. After the three of them had deliberated over the matter, the headman sent for Tisa.

'Mother of Isaki,' the headman began, 'as I promised you, I summoned your brother-in-law. This is a serious matter which requires to be considered by more than one head. So, I also invited Baba Nduna. Tell your brother-in-law in our presence every word that our father-in-law sent you to convey.'

Tisa presented the message from her father in detail.

'This is the message that he asked me to convey to my brother-in-law. He wants Baba Shuzi to go there at once so that he may discuss with him the boys' complaints. Those were my father's words, obaba,' Tisa concluded.

'Baba Shuzi, there is a case for you,' said headman Nkhanza.

'Hum,' muttered Shuzi. 'I am perplexed. Since when did people begin grabbing children from a man who paid malowolo?'

'My father did not grab those boys,' protested Tisa. 'They went there on their own accord.'

'Baba Shuzi,' said headman Nkhanza, 'we are not here to discuss whether our father-in-law followed tradition or not. I summoned you so that you could receive an important message. Our father-in-law is calling us for a meeting. We have to decide who will be accompanying you and when.'

'I agree with you, baba,' the nduna said. 'We have to send a delegation to Baba Lwando soon. Let us decide who will accompany Baba Shuzi. And when we have done that, we must work out what it is we will say to Baba Lwando.'

'What is there to say?' asked Shuzi. 'All that is required of us is to get there. Once we are there, it will be Baba Lwando's task to tell us what he called us for.'

'Baba Shuzi, you are taking this matter lightly. You have been summoned by your father-in-law in order that you may answer to charges of negligence. You are accused of failing in your duties as a father. We are here to assist you. In fact, you are embarrassing us by talking like that in the presence of mother of Isaki,' complained headman Nkhanza. And, turning to Tisa, he said, 'Mama, we have received the message. We can assure you that we will be sending a delegation there soon.'

There was silence as Tisa left the room. When they were certain that she had gone beyond earshot, the nduna spoke.

'Now that we are only men, I agree with Shuzi. Baba Lwando was wrong to keep our boys. When they complained about their father, he should have whipped them. By keeping them, he is making them stupid. Despite that, the fact remains that we are expected in Mtendere. I do not mind escorting Shuzi any day.'

'Those are words, Baba Nduna,' said headman Nkhanza. 'Now, let us think of what we will say to our father-in-law.'

'We will tell him that we have come to collect our boys,' said Shuzi.

'Baba Lwando could not have called you just for you to say, "I have come to collect my children." If all he wanted was someone to collect the boys, he would have let them come with their mother,' headman Nkhanza told Shuzi. 'You must be prepared to assure your father-in-law that you will not allow a situation whereby your children will run away from you again. You will have to promise that you will henceforth attend to all their needs. If you are not prepared to do that, then there will be no point in your going there. Those are my words.'

'And they are words, baba,' the nduna concurred.

'So, I will leave it to you both to agree on a day when you can go to Mtendere,' concluded headman Nkhanza.

As he left the headman's house, Shuzi was not a happy man. He blamed it all on Tisa. The boys would not have thought of going to Mtendere by themselves. She must have suggested it. Now he was expected to go down on his knees and make promises. How he wished he could refuse to co-operate! After all, it wasn't really his case. It was his brother's. If Musa had not left his wife and children in Nkhanza, this would not be happening.

A month later, Shuzi and the nduna honoured the summons from Lwando. After the greetings, Lwando went to alert headman Mtendere about their arrival. In the meantime, Shuzi wanted to see the two boys. He wanted to quiz them until they revealed who had advised them to leave Nkhanza without permission. But when he asked Mwaziona for the boys, her response shocked him.

'Your children are not here,' she told him. 'You know how crazy they are about school. Isaki left for Fort Jameson over a month ago. He went to secondary school. Yosefe also started school at Sairi. That one, at least, you will see when he comes home this afternoon,' Mwaziona said.

Shuzi and the nduna looked at each other, both of them speechless. Shuzi regretted having come. The problem was a lot bigger than he had imagined. So their father-in-law had gone as far as putting even Yosefe in school! Could he have given Isaki the fees? Nineteen pounds and fifteen shillings was too much for any villager.

The old man was pitting the boys against him. Now they would have an excuse for refusing to be in Nkhanza. They would say Mtendere was good for Yosefe because it was near his school. As for Isaki, he would claim that he had to spend his school holidays with his grandparents because that was where his fees came from. Shuzi did not feel like asking for the boys any longer. Doing so would be making a fool of himself. The matter was now beyond his control. He would have to go back to Nkhanza without the boys. Only his brother Musandivute could handle the issue.

Shuzi told the nduna his feelings. He wanted to leave Yosefe with his grandparents. He would write to Musandivute to tell him that he was no longer responsible for the two boys.

'This issue is becoming complex,' the nduna agreed. 'What is happening here is baffling. We should not attempt to collect Yosefe. That Baba Lwando put him in school shows that it was not his intention to let us take the boy. Let us leave the matter for Baba Musandivute to come and sort out.'

Lwando, headman Mtendere and his nduna had prepared

their strategy three weeks before. They needed only to put a few finishing touches to it. They were not going to mince their words. Headman Mtendere, who chaired the meeting, insisted that there was no need to conceal the truth from the men of Nkhanza.

'Obaba,' headman Mtendere began, 'we welcome you in this village. We are here to find out from you what the purpose of your visit is,' he said and stopped.

Shuzi looked at his nduna and the nduna looked at him. They had not anticipated that question. They had assumed that they would ask the first question. Shuzi was not only perplexed but quite vexed too.

The nduna to headman Nkhanza cleared his throat and began to speak. Shuzi gave him an accusing look as he opened his mouth but his nduna ignored him and went ahead with his response.

'Firstly, we bring you, obaba, good tidings from headman Nkhanza. We also bring you greetings from mother of Isaki,' he said and then paused. He wished someone would interrupt him for he was not sure whether to say what he had set out to say. But nobody did. Only silence reigned.

'You asked what we are here for. We came in response to the message which Baba Lwando sent to his son-in-law through mother of Isaki. The message was that Baba Lwando wanted Baba Shuzi to come so that they could discuss a problem regarding the two boys, Isaki and Yosefe. That, in short, obaba, is the purpose of our visit,' he said, feeling satisfied with himself.

Headman Mtendere and Lwando looked at each other and smiled.

'Is that all you came for?' asked headman Mtendere.

'Yes,' said Shuzi.

'That is strange,' remarked headman Mtendere. 'So, if your father-in-law had not sent for you, you would not have come?'

'No,' replied Shuzi.

'In that case, we do not have to proceed with this meeting,' said headman Mtendere. 'It is said that it is he that has stomach-ache who is expected to open the door. Your children ran away from you but you were not worried about where they were. And even after their mother told you they were here, you did not want to come for them. You are strange men. We thought you would have been looking for them from the day they went missing.'

'But knowing that the boys had left their village without permission, why did you not send them back?' asked Shuzi.

'Baba Shuzi,' said headman Mtendere, 'it seems you have problems in choosing your words. What we have here is a serious case of negligence. I suggest that you go back to Nkhanza and request your headman to give you real men to speak for you.'

'But I want to know where Isaki is.'

'That is your problem. Any responsible father ought to know where his children are at all times. You do not know the where-abouts of your own child because you do not want to. You do not care what happens to these children.'

'We do care, baba,' the nduna to headman Nkhanza pleaded.

'No, you don't,' the nduna to headman Mtendere concluded.

The following day, Shuzi and his nduna went back to Nkhanza. On arrival, they briefed headman Nkhanza about the outcome of their trip. When he was told all that had trans-pired, headman Nkhanza roared with laughter.

'Baba Shuzi, you do not want those children, do you? Why did you tell your father-in-law that you went there only because he summoned you?'

'What should I have said? He called me there.'

'No! You should have said you were there because you were concerned about your children. You should have said you were there to find out from your father-in-law why he was keeping the boys without your knowledge. You should have put it to him in such a way that it would have been him who had to defend himself. Now you have bungled. We have to think of another approach.'

'You mean we must go back to Mtendere?' asked Shuzi.

'Of course. How else do you think you will ever get those boys back? Do you want to lose them just like that?'

'I think my father-in-law is doing all this because he has a grudge against my brother. Perhaps there is something which only my brother and his father-in-law know. If not, perhaps there is something which mother of Isaki told her parents about us when she went there. Otherwise, why did she not come with the boys herself? Also, if Baba Lwando thought he would ever release the boys to me, why did he put them in school? Tisa and her father had already connived to ensure that the children would live in Mtendere. Do you not see that?'

'Baba Shuzi, you cannot win this battle if you begin to harbour such thoughts. Baba Lwando has caught you sleeping. Why did it take you so long to honour his summons? He will defend himself easily if you accuse him of putting your children in school. Was that not the major complaint that Isaki made against you? At the time the boys left this village, you had just refused to sell a bull for him to pay his fees. Well, his grandfather assisted you in that. He decided to pay the fees. As for Yosefe, perhaps he felt that you were only interested in making him look after your cattle.

'It will be difficult for you to win this case unless you admit that you have erred greatly. You will have to give your father-in-law a goat. And if you allow this matter to drag on so that it ends in court, you should not expect any sympathy from the chiefs. You know how much importance both Chief Nzamane and Chief Sairi place on children's education.'

'You know what I think, baba?' asked Shuzi. 'I think this case will be best handled by the courts. Baba Lwando wants to steal our children. No Ngoni chief will allow that to happen. No Ngoni chief will let a man keep both malowolo and the children for whom he charged and collected the malowolo.'

'Who will accompany you to court?' the nduna asked. 'Who do you think will want to witness untold humiliation there?'

'I am not asking you to come, Baba Nduna. If this case goes to court, my brother must come from Walale for it. After all, it is he who paid the malowolo that is at stake here. Only he knows the exact details of the deal he made with our father-in-law when he married mother of Isaki.'

'Baba Nduna, I think we need to give Baba Shuzi some time to reflect on the seriousness of this matter,' said headman Nkhanza. 'I doubt that he understands what a big case he has.'

'Those are words, baba,' the nduna assented.

'Baba Shuzi, we are not abandoning you. I know you need help. But take some time to think it over. You should also write to Baba Musandivute. Let him know all that has happened. Perhaps you should ask him to come to Nkhanza and see and hear for himself. Whenever you are ready to tackle the case again, you can come back to us. Those are my words.'

And the meeting ended there. From that day, nobody mentioned the matter to Shuzi. Nor did Shuzi discuss it with anybody in Nkhanza – not even with Tisa.

SIXTEEN

Musa had not written to Tisa for a long time and had not heard from her either. The last time he wrote to Northern Rhodesia was when Isaki asked for secondary school fees. He wondered what had become of him. Since his marriage to Rhoda, he had become more preoccupied with issues related to her and her immediate family than with Tisa and his seven children. His marriage to Rhoda and the subsequent arrival of their first child increased his expenses and took up a lot of his time.

The coming of their second daughter doubled Musa's expenditure. In the end, money was becoming so scarce that he dreaded getting any letter from Tisa or Isaki. What hurt him was that he was assumed to have a lot of money.

It was during this period that he received a letter from Shuzi. He read the letter whilst at work for he did not want Rhoda to learn about his problems in Northern Rhodesia.

26-10-1961

My dear father of Isaki,

How are you all there? Here, we are all well. The only problem is what I am writing this letter about. The trouble is that mother of Isaki does not listen to me. She behaves like a woman who has no husband.

I did not tell you earlier because I did not want to worry you. I had hoped that I would succeed in correcting her. I now regret it for things are out of control. Although mother of Isaki is still here, she is no longer answerable to me.

I am telling you all this because what she has done now is despicable. She has started moving the children from Nkhanza to her father in Mtendere. Right now, Isaki and Yosefe are not with me. They left for Mtendere four months ago. Our father-in-law sent Isaki to secondary school. I still have to find out who paid the fees. He also put Yosefe in school near their village. All that was done without consulting me.

That demoralised me for I had plans for Yosefe. I had wanted to bring him up in the same way that all Ngoni boys who have fathers are brought up. Now this will not happen as he is not here.

When I went to Mtendere to collect the boys, our father-in-law would not let me do so. Headman Mtendere told me that I did not know how to speak. He sent me back home to bring someone to speak for me. I did not think there was anybody in Nkhanza who could speak better than I about my own children. In fact, even on that trip I was not alone. The nduna accompanied me. And I tell you, the nduna knows how to speak. But headman Mtendere told him off too. So, if they would not listen to the nduna, I wonder who they would listen to.

You must come soon. Maybe our father-in-law will listen to you. But I do not think that the problem is with him. The real trouble is mother of Isaki. Maybe she is no longer interested in marriage. Come and find out for yourself from her why she is doing all this.

Please answer my letter soon.

I am your young brother of all times,

Shuzi.

Musa was infuriated and confused. He did not know who to blame for the entire situation. Was it Tisa or was it his father-in-law? But his father-in-law had always been on his side. What would have made him change his mind? Perhaps the dissension had been created by Shuzi. Maybe his brother had gone beyond his limits in expectations.

What troubled Musa's heart was how he would go about getting the truth of the matter. As his brother had suggested, the best thing would be for him to go to Nkhanza. The problem would be in connection with Rhoda. Would she be safe if left alone with two small children? Maybe he should try taking her and the children along. But that would be costly. And it would not be good for the children's health to make such a long journey.

125

There was also the problem of witchcraft. It was said that witches liked feasting on the tender bodies of babies of people just returned from Walale. He was not going to sacrifice his two daughters just because of problems created by villagers. Perhaps the best approach would be to discuss the matter with Rhoda and hear what she felt. Maybe she would have a splendid idea.

When he got home, his heart was troubled for he did not know how to start talking to Rhoda. He rarely discussed Tisa with her. He had learnt early in his marriage to Rhoda that she did not enjoy listening to him talk about her co-wife. But tonight, he did not have much choice. If he was going to travel to Northern Rhodesia, she had to know. And if he told her he had to go to Northern Rhodesia, he would have to tell her why.

'Will it be a good idea for me to travel to Northern Rhodesia?' Musa asked Rhoda after narrating the problem to her.

'I don't know.'

'What I mean is this, Rhoda. If I leave for Northern Rhodesia, will it be alright for you to remain in this house alone with the children?'

'You know I can't spend nights alone,' said Rhoda. 'Do you want thugs to attack us in the middle of the night?'

'Would you like to come to Northern Rhodesia with me, then?'

'Go to Northern Rhodesia, me? I have heard stories about witches in your country, especially in Fort Jameson. Many of the farm workers who are from there are afraid of going on leave. How much more afraid should I and my little girls be?'

'What do you suggest, then? You don't want to remain in the house and you don't want to come with me. So what do you want? Tell me if you have any better ideas.'

Rhoda laughed.

'Rhoda, is this a matter to laugh about? Don't you see that it is a serious problem? This is about my sons. My own sons have been taken away to a village which is not theirs. Don't you realise that it is humiliating for a man to lose his children like that? Remember, I paid malowolo for my children.'

'I know it is a serious matter,' said Rhoda.

'Why do you laugh then?'

'Do you expect me to decide for you what you must do about your wife? If you want to divorce her, that is up to you.'

'Who said anything about divorce? I'm concerned about my children and not about Tisa.'

'You don't have to be angry with me. I was only trying to answer your question.'

'But you haven't answered my question.'

'What is your question?'

'I wanted to know what you would do in my absence since you neither want to come with me nor remain in the house.'

'Well, if that's all you want to know, then I can only say that I'll go to my parents till you return.'

'That will be fine. We didn't have to quarrel about that when the solution was so simple,' said Musa.

'But you still have to find a reliable person to look after the house in our absence,' Rhoda told him.

'You're right. That is another obstacle, isn't it?' said Musa. But he did not get any response from her. And after that, he decided that it was no use trying to discuss the situation with her.

He thought the matter over before he fell asleep and he thought it over again the following day. In the end, he resolved that going all the way to Northern Rhodesia would not solve his problem. Thus, he settled on writing letters. He wrote letters to Tisa, Shuzi, Isaki and to his father-in-law. He enclosed the letter to his son in the envelope addressed to his father-in-law and that to his wife in the envelope addressed to his brother.

He told his son he had heard that he and Yosefe had left Nkhanza to live with their grandparents in Mtendere. He went on to castigate him for behaving in an unruly manner and ordered him and his young brother to return to Nkhanza at once. The letter to his wife had more or less the same tone as that to his son. He told her to go to Mtendere and bring the two boys back to Nkhanza immediately or he would lose his temper.

After writing the two short letters, he settled down to write to his brother and to his father-in-law in some detail.

My dear brother Shuzi,

How are you and everyone in the village? Here, we are all well. The only problem is that I am disturbed by what you wrote to me in your letter. Where were you when the two boys left Nkhanza? Why did you let them go? And when you went to Mtendere, why did you not take them back to Nkhanza with you?

It seems you are not interested in handling this issue. If that is the case, let me know and I will look for someone who is willing to help me.

If Tisa has not been listening to you, why have you done nothing about it? You could have brought her to a tribunal of elders. If that failed to change her, you could have sent her back to her parents in Mtendere so that they could teach her manners all over again.

What worries me is why these things happen to me as if I am the first man to leave a wife in the village. Many people have gone to work in the mines in South Africa or on the tobacco farms here or in the mines there in Northern Rhodesia, leaving one wife or two in the village. They have had no disturbing news from the village. Their brothers have looked after their wives and children the way they look after their own families. What makes it difficult for my own brother to help me in the same manner?

Bring those boys back to Nkhanza. If you have any trouble with Tisa, take any necessary disciplinary action that you would take against any of your own wives. When you answer my letter, I want to hear that you have taken the boys back and that Tisa has started behaving herself. I paid malowolo for my children. Why do you allow them to run away to their mother's village?

I am your elder brother of all times,
Musandivute.

When he finished writing that letter, he read it through and then put it in its envelope together with the one to his wife. Thereafter, he wrote to his father-in-law.

4-12-1961

My dear father-in-law,

How are you all there? Here, we are all well. I am pleased to inform you that we now have two daughters.

I am writing this letter to you because my brother has told me that your grandchildren, Isaki and Yosefe, ran away from Nkhanza and came to you. This has depressed me a lot. I wanted to come there to hear for myself but I have failed because V.V. will not allow me to take leave. However, I have written a letter to my brother in which I have told him to collect the children. Please, allow him to do so as he has my permission.

My brother is also complaining that mother of Isaki no longer listens to him. I feel Tisa is doing that deliberately in order to provoke me into divorcing her. She is my wife and I have no intention of divorcing her. Please, baba, ask elders in Mtendere to advise her to listen to my brother, for in my absence, he is her guardian as well as that of my children. I pray that by the time you answer my letter, these problems will have been solved. Please convey my greetings to my mother-in-law.

I am your son-in-law of all times,
Father of Isaki.

SEVENTEEN

At the end of the first term, Isaki was top of the 'A' stream and also top of the entire Form One. As soon as the results were released, news spread to the effect that a boy in Form One 'A' had scored one hundred per cent in mathematics. Getting every sum correct was not a minor achievement. It made the other boys appear stupid. But when they discovered which boy had done so well, they felt consoled. Every Form One boy knew Isaki as 'the boy without shoes'.

'Who is this fellow they say got one hundred out of one hundred in maths?' some boys would ask.

'The one without shoes,' would be the reply.

'Oh, no wonder!' they would say. 'No normal person can get everything correct in secondary school maths.'

His impressive performance at the end of the first term had coincided with other good news. The principal told him that the school had found him a two-year bursary.

'That should enable you to complete your junior school. After that, we are convinced that you should have no problem because if you continue to work hard, you should win a free place,' the principal told him.

When Lwando received the letter from Musa, Isaki had just come back home for the Christmas vacation. As his eyes were failing him, he asked his grandson to read the letter for him. After the letter was read, Lwando decided that he was not going to reply to it until he had talked to Shuzi. And since his son-in-law had told him in the letter that he had instructed his brother to collect the boys, it would not be necessary for Lwando to send a message for Shuzi to come over.

In the meantime, Shuzi, who had also received a letter from his brother, felt the most important point in the letter was the one which touched on the need to discipline Tisa. He loved that bit. Tisa deserved to be punished for trying to pit his brother's children against him. The most appropriate punishment would be to send her to her parents for good. That was the only disciplinary measure that she would appreciate. He replied to his brother's letter and advised him on that course of action.

13-1-62

My dear elder brother,

How are you? How are my sister-in-law and the children? Here, we are all well. The only problem is still mother of Isaki. She makes my heart burn with anger. Before your letter came, I did not know what to do. Now that you have told me to discipline her in any way I deem fit, I feel relieved.

Mother of Isaki has become so rude that no mere rebuke or beating will change her. The only thing that she can understand is divorce. I know that your white man may not allow you to come home. But do not let that make your heart burn with worry. You only have to authorise me to go ahead with the divorce. Once you have given me your permission, I will go to Chief Nzamane's court to start the divorce proceedings.

The chief will grant the divorce, for the crimes that mother of Isaki has committed are serious. No Ngoni chief will condone the behaviour of a woman who tells her husband's children to run away to her parents' home, more so where the man paid all the malowolo. Just write to me and I will do the rest.

As for the boys, do not let your heart ache. During the divorce hearings, I will make sure that the chief orders Baba Lwando to return them to us.

Pass my greetings to my sister-in-law.

I am your young brother of all times,
Shuzi.

Whilst Shuzi was thus waiting for his brother to give him permission to divorce Tisa on his behalf, his sister-in-law, having read and carefully considered the short letter from her husband, decided to consult headman Nkhanza. How could she fetch her sons from Mtendere when her father and the elders were still expecting a delegation from Nkhanza to go and finalise the matter? She wondered how Shuzi had put the issue across to his brother.

She was not going to fetch the boys and she was not going to answer her husband's letter. She would ask headman Nkhanza for advice. And she was not going to talk to her brother-in-law about it. She would let him write to his brother whatever he pleased. No matter how many lies Shuzi told him, she would not let it burn her heart for the Lord, who read every human being's mind, knew the truth. And some day, her husband would also know the truth.

Disturbed by the contents of Musa's letters, headman Nkhanza summoned Shuzi, Tisa, the nduna and other elders for a meeting.

'Obaba, I have called you here because mother of Isaki has told me that she has received a letter from her husband instructing her to fetch her sons back from her parents. We all know that those boys are supposed to be brought back here. We all want them to come back because this is where they belong,' said headman Nkhanza and then paused.

'What worries me is this, obaba,' he continued. 'If our own children run away from us, it is our duty to follow them and find out what has made them do that. It is our duty to go and fetch them. It is not the duty of women. Therefore, it is unfair, and unwise too, for us to allow mother of Isaki to do this duty for us,' he said and paused again.

'What I would like to know is, who wrote to Baba Musandivute about this? Baba Musandivute probably thinks we have refused to help him. Otherwise, he would not have ordered his wife to perform a task which is meant for us men. Who wrote to him about this?' he asked. And eyes turned to Shuzi.

Shuzi coughed once and began to speak.

'Obaba, allow me to explain. I wrote to my brother because I believed that this problem required his presence. I told him all that happened and advised him to come here and sort out the matter for himself. But my brother told me that he could not come because his white man would not grant him leave,' said Shuzi.

'Now, do you see what problem you have created for mother of Isaki?' asked headman Nkhanza. 'And it is not only mother of Isaki whom you are bothering. Your brother's heart is also troubled. When your brother is so far away from home, you must not tell him every problem that you face with his wife or children. It is your responsibility to solve those problems without writing to him. That is why he left them with you. Now, tell us how you will get out of this mess,' headman Nkhanza challenged Shuzi.

'Obaba, why do you treat me as if I caused all this to happen?' complained Shuzi.

'Do you now want to wash your hands of this matter, Baba Shuzi?' the nduna asked. 'This is your case. In the absence of your elder brother, this matter is wholly your responsibility.'

'Are you implying that I am trying to shy away from my responsibilities? I am not a coward. We all know the real culprit. This whole problem was created by mother of Isaki.'

'Ha!' Tisa exclaimed.

'Yes,' continued Shuzi. 'If it were not for your stubbornness, we would not be here. You advised those boys to go to your parents.'

'Obaba, we have been through this before,' said Tisa. 'My brother-in-law knows that I did not tell those boys to go to my parents. He is saying all this because he knows that he has been a failure. He has not looked after my children the way a caring father is expected to.'

'Do you see what I mean, obaba?' Shuzi interjected. 'Who expects a woman to say such things against her husband's brother? I am tired of this woman.'

'Baba Shuzi,' intervened headman Nkhanza, 'you have not answered my question.'

'What was your question?'

Everybody laughed.

'What do you want to do about this whole issue now?'

'I will do as my brother says. If he tells me to divorce her, I will do it. I am not as cowardly as some of you think. I am tired of being summoned to the headman's house as if I am the only man in this village who has marital problems.'

'If that is what you want, you can divorce me tomorrow. We will see what the court will say to you,' Tisa retorted.

'Mother of Isaki, do not say such things,' pleaded headman Nkhanza. 'I did not call all these obaba in order to destroy. I called everyone here because I want us to build. Divorce is something that only cowards resort to. Now, since Baba Shuzi is showing signs of anger, it is best that we adjourn. When his heart has cooled down a little, we will reconvene. We should still send a delegation to Baba Lwando. He is expecting us,' headman Nkhanza concluded and dismissed them all.

The letter from Shuzi depressed Musa. How could he suggest that he divorce Tisa? Musa did not want to divorce her. Maybe his brother had his own grudge against her. It was necessary that he wrote to him immediately.

10-2-62

My dear brother Shuzi,

I have received the letter you sent me on 13-1-62. Do not think of divorcing Tisa. She is my wife for whom I paid both cimalo and malowolo. Even if I die, Tisa must remain in that village with all my sons. Those are my only words to you.

I am your brother of all times,
Musandivute.

Shuzi tore up the letter. He did not want anybody to know what his brother had told him. If they did, they would laugh at him. Now that his brother had adopted that attitude, Shuzi would have nothing to do with his wife. He would let her do as she pleased. She could even go off with any man in front of his eyes and he would say nothing about it. As for the two boys, Musa would have to come for them himself or be prepared to lose them. Shuzi would not go for them. And he was not going to respond to his brother's letter.

After waiting several weeks in vain for Shuzi and his people to call on him, Lwando decided to answer his son-in-law's letter.

19-5-1962

My dear father of Isaki,

Greetings to you and your family. I apologise for taking so long to answer your letter. I wanted to have the chance to speak to Baba Shuzi before writing to you. I was hoping that after I had met with him and my fellow elders from Nkhanza, I might have something concrete to tell you.

I have been informed by mother of Isaki that Baba Shuzi has refused to come and see me. I have also been told that he is waiting for a letter from you authorising him to divorce mother of Isaki on your behalf.

Mother of Isaki has been a good wife to you for so many years and she has given you seven children. If you want to divorce her, do so in a respectful manner. I beg you to come so that we can sort out this problem. Isaki and Yosefe are still under my care and will remain so until you come to see me about them.

Pass my greetings to my friend V.V.

I am your father-in-law of all times,

Lwando.

EIGHTEEN

In May 1963, Isaki sat for the Junior Secondary School Certificate exam. The exam was crucial for him because his aim was to pass well enough to win a free place for his senior school. He had no money to pay for his education but he had a lot of faith, for indeed, all good things came from the Lord. He felt encouraged by the testimony in the Book of James chapter one, verse seventeen, wherein it is said:

> *Every good and perfect gift is from above, coming down from the Father of the heavenly lights, who does not change like shifting shadows.*

When the Junior Secondary School Certificate results were released, Isaki was jubilant and praised the Lord. He had obtained six distinctions and two credits. That earned him a free place for the next three years. When Isaki got the results, he and Yosefe were with their grandparents.

A fortnight earlier, the two brothers and their grandparents had been pleased because Yosefe had qualified for Standard Three. Following in his elder brother's footsteps, Yosefe would be leaving Sairi Lower Primary School to join Angoni Upper School. Like his elder brother, his Standard Two examination results were the best in the school that year. The headmaster, who was initially reluctant to admit him into Sub B, was later so impressed with the boy's performance that in the same year, he had promoted him from Sub B to Standard One. And now, two years later, Yosefe qualified for Standard Three.

At the same time, Isaki not only qualified for Form Three but won a free place for Forms Three, Four and Five. It was a happy moment for the two boys and their grandparents. There was, however, one hurdle. Yosefe would require nine pounds and fifteen shillings for his boarding-school fees. But the boys did not allow that to dampen their spirits. Isaki assured his younger brother that all would be well.

In their joy, the boys paid their mother a surprise visit. 'Do not worry about fees, my children,' Tisa told them. 'The Lord will provide. Nine pounds and fifteen shillings is a lot of money but nothing is impossible with our heavenly Father. In the meantime, there is something we can do. I have harvested some groundnuts. If we shell a bagful, we can make three pounds. The headmaster would accept a deposit of three pounds.'

'He would accept three pounds and five shillings,' said Isaki.

'If we made three pounds from the sale of groundnuts, five shillings would not be too much to raise from other sources. We could even borrow it,' suggested Yosefe.

The next day, the family got down to the business of shelling groundnuts. They shelled groundnuts in the morning, in the afternoon and in the evening until their fingers developed blisters. After two weeks, they filled up a bag with groundnuts of a grade which they reckoned would be acceptable to the co-operative union that bought farm produce from peasant farmers.

Then came their next problem. They did not have oxen to take their bag to the co-operative union market. They had no bicycle either. If they had one, Isaki and Yosefe could have ferried the groundnuts in small loads.

'Baba Shuzi has an ox-cart,' their mother told them, 'and some of the oxen he uses belong to your father. But if you asked him, he would not lend it to you.'

'Why don't we try him?' asked Yosefe.

'That's a good idea,' Isaki concurred.

'No!' their mother objected.

'Why not?' asked Yosefe.

'You know that he will not agree,' said their mother.

'Mother, he may surprise you,' said Isaki.

'Well, if you insist, who am I to say "no"? After all, he is your father. But when you ask him, do not mention my name. You know how much he hates me.'

Shuzi was seated in the corridor of his senior wife's house when Isaki and Yosefe approached him. When he saw them, he sighed in disgust. The sight of them angered him. It was because of these two boys that relations between him and his elder brother had soured. How he wished he could whip them back to their mother's house!

The boys politely announced their arrival and sat down at a little distance. Then, they waited for a greeting. After waiting quietly for some time, the boys became restless.

'Baba,' Isaki began, 'we are here to ask you for some help.'

'What sort of help?' asked Shuzi.

'We need an ox-cart to take a bag of groundnuts to the market.'

'Listen here. I do not want to lend you my ox-cart. If you need one, go to your grandfather and ask him.'

The boys sat there quietly for a moment.

'Go away!' Shuzi shouted.

Yosefe rose and walked away towards his mother's house. But Isaki sat there and looked Shuzi straight in his angry face.

'What are you staring at me like that for? Go to your mother. I will not let you use my ox-cart. You are not my children any more.'

'Well, if you say so, it will be alright with us,' said Isaki. 'But you cannot stop us from using the ox-cart because the oxen that pull it are ours.'

'Is that what your mother tells you? Let me tell her the truth loudly enough for the whole village to hear,' he said as he walked towards Tisa's compound.

Isaki rose and walked after him.

'Mother of Isaki!' Shuzi called. 'You woman without a head,' he shouted at her, 'listen to me carefully. You may be wondering why I am shouting at you. Perhaps you want to know why I did not ask a child to call you to my house so that I could talk to you quietly, the way a man is expected to talk to the wife of his elder brother. I have to shout across to you because I would like everyone to hear what I have to say.'

Shocked, Tisa walked towards her brother-in-law.

'No!' shouted Shuzi. 'Do not come to my compound. Listen to me from the confines of your own home,' he ordered. Turning to

Isaki who was standing behind him, he said, 'You too. Leave my compound at once! Go to your mother.'

Quite a few people had come out of their homes to watch.

'You and your two sons have done me a lot of harm. From this moment, I want to have nothing to do with you. You are no longer my sister-in-law and your children are no longer my children,' he announced. Then, leaving all his listeners in suspense, he walked to a rubbish dump where he fetched a long stick. The onlookers gasped with a mixture of fear and astonishment. Was he going to whip Tisauke and her children with that stick? Her youngest children ran into the house, crying.

'So, you want to kill us!' retorted Tisa. 'Alright, come and kill us so that you may enjoy eating the flesh of our bodies.'

'I am not going to beat you. Stand where you are and watch what I am about to do. I am going to draw a boundary between your compound and mine. Neither you and your children nor my wives, my children and I may cross this barrier to go into the compound of the other from now until we die. If I cross this frontier to come to your compound, may lightning strike me dead. If any members of my family cross this boundary into your compound, may they too be struck by lightning. And should you, mother of Isaki, or any of your children, cross this line to come over here, may lightning strike you dead. Watch this,' he told them and then drew a line separating his compound from Tisa's.

From that moment, there was to be no communication between the two families. Everyone knew the seriousness of njazi. People who swore never to be in any form of contact with each other by invoking the wrath of lightning knew it was no mere game. Njazi was no joke. So, as soon as Shuzi had drawn that barrier line between them, nobody said another word. They all withdrew to their respective homes. Even the onlookers did not say anything. But Isaki and Yosefe decided that what Shuzi had done would have no adverse effect on them.

'Don't worry, mother,' Isaki said to her. 'We don't need that man. We have never needed him. We'll manage with the help of our Father in heaven.'

139

They had an idea about how they would take their bag of groundnuts to the market. They would ferry the groundnuts in baskets. They did not mind how many trips they made nor how long it took. Their mother helped them. They each carried a basket on their heads.

It was not customary for a male to carry a basket on his head. Men and boys were not expected to carry anything, let alone baskets on their heads. They were supposed to carry things on their right shoulders. Any boy who carried anything on his head was pitied, for it was feared that he would grow up to be not quite a man. But neither Isaki nor his young brother minded what people thought.

Isaki knew what he wanted to be. He did not mind whether people thought he would grow up to be half man and half woman. He did not want to be a woman. He did not want to be a mere man either. Growing up to be a man did not require any brains. Everyone born a boy would grow up to be some kind of man. He was determined to be more than just a man. Isaki was going to be a medical doctor. So, he made those trips to the market with a basket on his head.

In the end, they sold a bagful of groundnuts for three pounds. And they had a tin of groundnuts left over which they sold for ten shillings. Before school opened, Isaki escorted his younger brother to Angoni Upper School to negotiate for him to be admitted after paying three pounds and five shillings as a deposit on his fees. On arrival at Angoni, Isaki knew that there would be no problem for Mr Ndlovu, the headmaster he had left two years earlier, was still there. And indeed, Mr Ndlovu accepted that arrangement.

A few days before school opened, the two brothers went back to Mtendere where they thanked their grandparents for having looked after Yosefe for two years. Thereafter, they said farewell and promised to visit them during their school holidays.

NINETEEN

Nineteen sixty-three was a special year for the British Protectorate of Northern Rhodesia as the country was granted self-government. Kenneth Kaunda became its first Prime Minister.

One of the first fruits of that achievement was in the field of education. Harry Nkhumbula, who had just become Minister of Education in the United National Independence Party – African National Congress coalition government, announced two changes in the education system. Firstly, there was going to be a change in the school calendar. The academic year would, with effect from 1964, start in mid-January and end in early December.

The immediate effect of that change was the shortening of that academic year to six months, that is, from July to December 1963. School pupils all over the country loved it.

That was not all. The Minister further announced that the primary school course would be shortened by one year. Instead of having Sub A, Sub B and Standards One to Six, the new system would consist of Grades One to Seven.

Isaki and Yosefe welcomed that change. It was going to help them financially. To start with, it meant that for the July-December 1963 academic year, they did not have to worry about raising nine pounds and fifteen shillings for Yosefe's boarding-school fees. That year, the primary school boarding fees were reduced to six pounds and ten shillings. Secondly, it meant that Yosefe would be completing primary school one and a half years earlier. Isaki thanked God for those changes. They only needed to look for three pounds and five shillings to complete Yosefe's fees for Standard Three which had now been designated as Grade Five.

When they returned to Nkhanza for their holiday, Isaki and Yosefe thought of ways to raise the remaining three pounds and five shillings for Yosefe's fees. But it was not an easy task. Their mother had no groundnuts left for sale. Even if she did, they would have nowhere to sell them as the market season for the co-operative union was over.

They did not dare ask Shuzi. Talking to him would be as good as committing suicide on account of the njazi between them. They did not want to write to their father either. They had lost all confidence in him. It was high time they understood that he was a real muchona. He had not responded positively to Isaki's requests for fees in the past. And there was nothing to indicate that he would respond differently this time.

It was their grandmother who had a practical idea. She knew a number of regular drinkers of kachasu. She would brew some and offer it to them for sale. Of course, what she could brew at one time might not raise the required amount but if she promised to brew a few more bottles for them in the near future, they would lend her the remaining cash.

It was customary for some government departments and private companies to offer vacation employment to senior secondary school pupils. In Fort Jameson, however, opportunities for such jobs were limited. Many boys and girls who had relatives in Lusaka and the Copperbelt towns sent several applications to as many of these towns as they could. Isaki needed such a job to raise fees for Yosefe for the 1964 academic year as well as some pocket money for himself. But he had two problems.

Firstly, he did not have relations in Lusaka or on the Copperbelt and so he could only apply for a job in Fort Jameson. Secondly, he did not have money for postage stamps. In order to increase one's chances, the tradition was to send out several application letters. Isaki could not afford that. He prayed for God's assistance. At a time when most of his colleagues sent out dozens of application letters, Isaki decided to write only one. To minimise competition, he chose an organisation which he felt was not popular with school pupils. Something told him that the Fort Jameson Township Board would do for him.

When he finished writing the letter, he thought of how he would get it to the Secretary of the Fort Jameson Township Board since he had no money for a postage stamp. After a little thinking, he reckoned he could take it by hand. So he went to the boarding-master to ask for permission to go into town.

'What do you want to do in town during the week?' the boarding-master asked him.

'I want to take an application letter for a vacation job.'

'You don't have to take it in person,' the boarding-master told him. 'You must post it. That is what they expect you to do.'

'I know that, sir, but I have no stamp, sir.'

The boarding-master offered him one.

A week later, the boarding-master summoned him to his office and told him that he had received a telephone call from the Secretary of the Fort Jameson Township Board.

'He wants you to see him in connection with your application for a vacation job,' the boarding-master told him. And he gave him permission to go to town for that purpose.

When Isaki got there, he found four girls from a neighbouring secondary school also waiting to see the Secretary of the Fort Jameson Township Board. Because of the girls' presence, Isaki waited for most of that afternoon. The Secretary of the Fort Jameson Township Board was unable to see Isaki until after he had seen the last of the four girls. Before his turn to be ushered in, Isaki learnt that none of the girls had been offered a job. That made him panic. He wondered what sort of questions had been asked that they had failed to answer. This being his first job interview, Isaki was nervous.

Before he went into the Secretary's office, he said a short prayer, asking God to help him perform well in the interview.

Contrary to his expectations, the Secretary of the Fort Jameson Township Board was not a fat man with a thick neck and a huge tummy. He was even more astonished when the man began by asking him ordinary questions.

'How is school?'

'It's going on well, sir.'

'In your letter, you said you need a vacation job in order to raise school fees for your younger brother.'

'Yes, sir.'

'Don't you have a father who can pay your brother's fees?'

'I do, sir. But he is a muchona. He is in Southern Rhodesia and he does not write to us any longer. I don't know why, sir.'

'What about your own fees? Who is going to pay for you?'

'I don't pay fees, sir. I won a free place for my senior secondary school.'

'Congratulations!'

'Thank you, sir.'

'You also said that you are prepared to do any kind of job. Did you mean it?'

'Yes, sir.'

'If I told you that the only job available at the moment is emptying dustbins, would you take it?'

'Oh, certainly! I would take it, sir. I have never done that kind of job before but I'm sure I could learn from those who have been doing the job a long time.'

The Secretary of the Fort Jameson Township Board paused and smiled at him. Thereafter, he picked up the phone and dialled some number.

'Hello! Is that the Clerk of Works? Oh, how are you this afternoon? That's good. I have a schoolboy in my office. From Chizongwe? Yes, he is. Yes. What sort of work? Anything. He says he is prepared to do any kind of work. Good! I'll send him over to you. Certainly not today. He should see you tomorrow? Okay, I'll tell him. Thank you. Bye!'

'That's it!' said the Secretary of the Fort Jameson Township Board to Isaki when he had replaced the telephone receiver on its hook. 'You have a vacation job. Report to the Clerk of Works tomorrow afternoon. He'll give you the details.'

The Clerk of Works was also not as huge as Isaki had expected. Isaki liked the fact that so far, he had dealt with small-bodied superiors because he did not feel intimidated by their sheer physical appearance.

'Is it true that you are prepared to do any kind of job?' the Clerk of Works asked him.

'Yes, sir.'

'That is strange. Boys from your school who have applied for jobs in the Board before have refused to do manual work. But the nature of our work in this department does require the use of our hands. In spite of your willingness to do any sort of job, I have decided to give you one that befits a senior secondary schoolboy like you. You'll work in our storeroom under the supervision of the stores clerk. With him, you'll be responsible for issuing tools and spare parts to our workers every day. You'll also be responsible for ordering such tools and parts. The work involves keeping a record of items received and those issued. I'm sure you'll easily learn what is involved.'

At the end of that academic year, Isaki did not go home for the holidays but spent six weeks working in the Works Department of the Fort Jameson Township Board. He had a six-day week with Saturday as a half day. He liked the job from the first day mostly because his immediate supervisor was a pleasant man. He also looked forward to getting the money at the end of that vacation.

Isaki's daily wages were fixed at twelve shillings and six pence. To ensure that he earned the maximum amount for that period, he was determined not to be absent from work for any reason other than illness. In the end, Isaki reported for work on each of the thirty-six working days during that vacation. He was given twenty-two pounds and ten shillings at the end of his holiday job. That was the biggest sum of money that he had ever had in his life. When he got it, he went home and sat down to draw up his first budget ever.

After getting his wages, Isaki was free to spend the last few days of his vacation in his village. But he did not go home. He wanted to be at work for two more days to show his appreciation for the opportunity he had been given to earn his own cash for the first time in his life. He also wanted to say farewell to his immediate supervisor, the stores clerk, as well as to the Clerk of Works and the Secretary of the Township Board. Each of the three men spoke highly of him and assured him that he would be welcomed again during his school holidays in future.

TWENTY

Since taking over from his father-in-law as foreman, Musa had acquired many responsibilities. From the start, he was given the responsibility of recruiting labourers from Northern Rhodesia and Nyasaland. Because he recruited the majority of the labourers and because they believed that he had been fortified by a malevolent witch-doctor at Nchisi in Nyasaland, he was revered by everyone. The rumour about his having been boiled alive in a mixture of herbs and roots contributed greatly to his undisputed authority.

For some time, he was regarded as the third highest at the farm after V.V. and his son. Later, when V.V.'s son opted for a teaching job, V.V. elevated his position to that previously held by his son. That elevation neatly coincided with his marriage to the young and relatively schooled Rhoda. V.V. finally crowned that promotion by letting him move into the house that was formerly his son's. Musa became pikinini baas.

His authority grew as V.V. advanced in age. The older V.V. became, the less involved he was in the day-to-day running of the farm. Eventually, he reduced his role to the extent that his son became concerned. In his son's opinion, there were some roles which no African pikinini baas could perform well, no matter how hard-working he might be. V.V.'s son was supported by his mother, the misisi herself. She advised him to make surprise visits to the farm. Each time he came, he would travel from one tobacco plot to another on horseback.

The labourers loathed the days when he came because he made them work longer hours. But Musa detested such days even more. Those visits would eventually undermine his authority. But there was nothing he could do, especially since V.V.'s son was doing it all with the blessing of the misisi. Musa feared the misisi. The woman seldom talked to him. Now that V.V. was seen more rarely outside his house, Musa had less access to him. Each time he went to his house, he would be greeted by a pack of ferocious dogs. Thereafter, the misisi would emerge and ask him what he wanted. Occasionally, she would call V.V. out but on other occasions, she would take messages to and from him. Musa resented that. All he could do was look back with nostalgia to the days when he and V.V. walked abreast from one end of a tobacco plot to another.

A more devastating blow to Musa's authority manifested itself when V.V. Junior began to spend vacations from his teaching job at the farm. He would run the show from sunrise to sunset. Musa's day started at five in the morning when he would ring the bell for all the workers to report at their various places of work. It would end at four in the afternoon when he would again ring the bell to signal knocking-off time. He loved these two chores. They gave him a sense of authority. But during the days when V.V. Junior was at the farm, he would deprive him of this responsibility. V.V. Junior would ring the bell before the official hour of five in the morning. Musa resented that. He did not mind the fact that the workers were made to start work earlier than usual. What bothered him was that it had not been he who had made them get up that early but someone else.

These incidents made Musa begin to think seriously about his future. He thought of what he would do in Northern Rhodesia when he retired from work. One possibility was to run a small shop near his village. He had the perfect spot in mind where he could build one, at Katawa bus stop. And after making a little money from the shop, he would venture into farming. In Northern Rhodesia, land was cheaper than it was in Southern Rhodesia. He could afford it. Besides, initially, he would do some farming on a small scale. That way, he would not need much land. He would get such land free of charge from the chief. He would buy land at a later stage when he needed to expand the farm.

But two issues worried him. A business was best run in partnership with one's sons. What was happening at V.V.'s farm was a good pointer to that. Here was V.V. letting his son run the farm now that he was ageing himself. If V.V. had no son, his ageing may have led to the virtual collapse of the farm. Musa wondered what would happen to his envisaged shop and farm in his old age. He had four sons in Northern Rhodesia but lately, there had been no contact between him and them. He did not even know whether they were in Nkhanza or in Mtendere.

And Tisa? What could have become of her? He shuddered to think how he would feel if he returned to Nkhanza only to find that she had long divorced him and left with all the children. Of course, he had other children from Rhoda. But these were both girls. He wouldn't rely on daughters because they would eventually get married and join their husbands. It was for that reason that he would have loved to have at least one son from Rhoda. But Rhoda did not want to have any more children. There was nothing he could do about it. They had not considered the matter at the time of their courtship.

Perhaps his only solution was to resume contact with his sons and Tisa. In fact, wouldn't it be best if he travelled to Northern Rhodesia? Maybe his father-in-law was still waiting for him to sort out the problem regarding his two sons. But there remained the issue of where Rhoda would stay during the period that he was away in Northern Rhodesia. Even if he sorted that out, would V.V. grant him leave at a time when he needed him more due to his feeble disposition? And assuming that he let him go, could Musa tell what changes V.V.'s son could make at the farm during his absence?

He had to do something about it. He would have to face Rhoda to discuss the possibility of his taking leave to go to Northern Rhodesia. Besides his wish to sort out his family problems, there was also the need to see what was happening in his country. People who came from there brought many stories. It was said that the country had been granted self-government and that at any time, it would get full independence. There would be a black government. Kenneth Kaunda was expected to be the first president and he would choose a team of black Africans as ministers. He wondered what kind of government it would be. If he went on leave, he would see it all with his own eyes.

On 24 October 1964, Northern Rhodesia attained full political independence from Great Britain. Celebrations were held countrywide. In Fort Jameson, people gathered from all over the Eastern Province on the afternoon of 23 October. The singing and dancing was to go on until midnight when the country would become independent. At exactly midnight, Northern Rhodesia would become Zambia and Sir Evelyn Hone would cease to be the British Governor of the country. Instead, Kenneth Kaunda would become Zambia's first president. The whole country was excited. Everybody was proud to have their own man, a black Zambian, as head of state. The whole country couldn't wait. From that moment, the photograph of Queen Elizabeth II and that of Sir Evelyn Hone, Governor of Northern Rhodesia, would come down from the walls of every public building. In their place, up would go the portrait of Kenneth David Kaunda. From exactly midnight, they would no longer sing 'God Save the Queen'. They would henceforth 'Stand and Sing of Zambia, Proud and Free'. That was the meaning of independence.

At Chizongwe Secondary School, every boy was excited. Isaki could not wait for midnight. A lot had been said about the good that was to come with independence. Kenneth Kaunda had summed it all up by declaring that come independence, every Zambian would have no less than one pair of shoes and eat at least one egg a day.

For Isaki, that bit about the shoes said it all. If independence would enable every citizen to have no less than one pair of shoes, then that independence had better come fast. He recalled that during his first two years at Chizongwe, he had earned the nickname 'the boy without shoes' because, indeed, he had none. He did not mind whether he had an egg a day or not. He had eaten several eggs in his life. But shoes! He had bought his first pair only at the beginning of that year.

That evening of 23 October 1964, Isaki, like the rest of the boys at Chizongwe, was excited. The climax of that excitement came a couple of minutes before midnight, at the Beit Stadium in Fort Jameson. There was a great multitude of people, all waiting patiently for midnight when the entire country would undergo the transformation from Northern Rhodesia to Zambia.

The singing and dancing stopped. Lights were all turned off except for one at the top end of the flag-pole. Total silence descended. At the very top of the flag-pole hung the Union Jack and on the ground, at the foot of the pole, lay the brand new flag of the Republic of Zambia, ready for the moment when it would start the upward movement towards independence.

At a pre-arranged time, at every such centre in the entire country, the two flags started their respective journeys. Cautiously, the Union Jack started to come down at exactly the same moment as the Zambian flag started to move majestically upward. The entire country stood at attention. Watching the two flags, Isaki could see all his problems evaporate and all his ambitions materialise before his own eyes.

And indeed, at exactly midnight, the Union Jack dropped to the ground as the green Zambian flag simultaneously sprouted into life at the top of the flag-pole. Lights were turned on, drums beat, fireworks exploded and lit up the sky with a variety of colours, and there followed great jubilation from the multitudes. The Zambian nation had just been born!

Isaki wondered what his father in Southern Rhodesia thought about the independence which had come to his motherland. Southern Rhodesia was still a British colony but with its northern neighbour independent and having acquired a brand new name, Southern Rhodesia was no longer to be Southern Rhodesia. It was to be called Rhodesia.

The new government of Kenneth Kaunda introduced many changes. It made it clear that it placed a great deal of importance on education, agriculture and health. Isaki loved the fact that what Chief Sairi Three had told them some eight years earlier was what the new government was telling the nation. He wished he could see Chief Sairi Three again to tell him how much he appreciated his words of 1956. He wished he could say to him, 'Education is the key,' over and over again. He was sure that wherever the chief was, he must be happy to see that education was given such a top priority by the new government.

One of the changes in the field of education was going to be the establishment of a national university in Lusaka. Another change was that the government had decided to abolish Form Six. This meant that deserving people would enter university immediately after their 'O' levels.

That pleased Isaki. He could now smell his career in medicine. In less than two years, he would be at the University of Zambia as one of its pioneering students. There, he would study medicine and be one of its first medical graduates seven years later. And he would not forget to encourage his young brother to study hard too. Now that he had been assured of a job every vacation, he would be able to raise Yosefe's school fees.

Twelve months later, Isaki took the Cambridge School Certificate examinations. At about the same time, Yosefe was to take the primary school-leaving examinations. In that year, the government brought about another change in the education system. From 1966, free education would be introduced. That meant all academically eligible citizens and residents of Zambia would henceforth attend school without paying any tuition or boarding fees. Free education was extended to all tertiary institutions of learning, including the University of Zambia.

Isaki thanked God for that development. No longer would he worry his mother about fees. No longer would he send his father those demanding letters. If he ever wrote to his father again, it would be to find out how he was getting on. Or it would be to tell him how he and Yosefe were doing – just to prove to him that education was, indeed, the key.

The primary school-leaving examination results were released earlier than the school certificate results. Once again, following in the footsteps of his elder brother, Yosefe qualified for a place at Chizongwe Secondary School. Unlike his elder brother, however, he did not have to worry about where his school fees would come from. He needed only to find the sum of five pounds for his uniforms.

Unlike his elder brother's days at Chizongwe, the headmaster had not sent a long list of items to be brought to school. As for shoes, it was assumed that every school-going child, if not every

Zambian, had no less than one pair. Hadn't independence brought shoes and eggs closer to the people? Also unlike his elder brother, Yosefe would not be walking the twenty-five miles to Fort Jameson. He would have enough money for the bus and some cash for his pocket. His brother Isaki would provide it because he had a vacation job at the Fort Jameson Township Board.

Two months later, the school certificate results were also released. Isaki obtained a first division pass. With eighteen points, he easily qualified for the University of Zambia. He would be admitted into the School of Natural Sciences during his first two years. Depending on his performance in the end-of-year examinations, he would proceed to the School of Medicine where he would spend five years studying what he had dreamed of since leaving Angoni Upper Primary School.

Musa decided to take a short leave. He wanted to travel to his home country for three reasons. Firstly, he was anxious to see what changes independence had brought. He had heard that the country was no longer called Northern Rhodesia. He wanted to experience the difference between Northern Rhodesia and Zambia. He did not want to rely on what other people said. Secondly, he wanted to explore the possibility of his starting a small business at Katawa bus stop. And lastly, he was keen to re-assemble his family.

When he approached V.V. for the leave, he was told that he should wait until V.V. Junior came to the farm for his next school holidays. V.V. did not want to leave the farm without any leadership. It would be best for Musa to leave when V.V. Junior was around. And so, he waited. When V.V. Junior came, V.V. referred Musa's request for leave to him.

'No, he can't go,' said V.V. Junior.

'Why not?' asked V.V.

'Don't you know what's happening? The border between Rhodesia and Zambia is closed. If he attempts to go, he may not be able to cross the Zambezi. If he does manage to cross, he will never come back,' V.V. Junior explained to his father.

'So that independence of theirs won't do us any good,' commented V.V.

'Not at all. But the problem is not due to their independence. The cause of the problem is our so-called independence,' remarked V.V. Junior.

'Why do you say that? Are you out of your mind?'

'I am not. I feel Ian Smith should not have declared independence unilaterally last year. He should have accepted the British government's proposals for settlement. If he had done that, we would have continued to enjoy peace. Now we'll have to put up with acts of terrorism.'

'You mean whites should have given in to the demands made by the so-called African nationalists?' asked V.V.

'Why not?'

'That would be the end of our political and economic dominance.'

'But we would not lose our property. Whilst they would be contented with some political power, we would happily keep the land and our wealth to ourselves. But now the United Nations is talking of imposing economic sanctions against this country. And the border with our northern neighbour is closed.'

'That worries me,' said V.V. 'My farm has always depended on cheap labour from Northern Rhodesia and Nyasaland. Now, I can't expect any more recruits from those countries, can I?'

'I'm afraid you can't. You'll have to retain the labourers you have at the moment. That includes your foreman. If you let any one of them go, you could trigger a whole exodus. You know, these stories they hear about what is going on in their countries could easily lure them away from here.'

Following this chat with his son, V.V. discouraged Musa from ever contemplating travelling to his country.

'Foreman, don't ever think of going to Northern Rhodesia again,' V.V. advised Musa.

'Why not, Baas?'

'It is neither possible nor safe to do so. Firstly, the border between the two countries is closed. Secondly, it is likely that there will be acts of terrorism along the borders, especially from that other end.'

'But Baas, it is important that I visit my misisi and the children. I haven't seen them for ten years,' Musa pleaded.

'I know, foreman, and I sympathise, but I tell you it isn't possible for you to go at the moment. You must wait for the situation to get better.'

Musa accepted that advice. He hadn't much choice. If he went against his baas's wishes, he would do so at his own risk. To start with, he would have to raise his own money for the trip. Secondly, during his absence, V.V.'s son might replace him. Musa was not going to take that chance. At least if he left with V.V.'s blessing, he could expect some protection from his son's wrath.

TWENTY-ONE

Being a student at the University made Isaki appreciate more the meaning of independence. He did not have to pay any fees and did not even have to know how much it was going to cost the government to keep him there. The government was also going to give the students pocket money and transport money every term. Students also had a book allowance.

Besides those generous hand-outs, something else made the university a good place. The food was excellent and so was the service. All you did was walk to the dining-hall and find yourself a table, and a waiter would be at your service.

One other thing that Isaki appreciated was the fact that you didn't have to go to the dining-hall if you didn't want to. Eating was not a compulsory activity. This contrasted markedly with Angoni Upper School where it was not only obligatory that you report for every meal but also compulsory that you finish all the food that you found on your plate.

At the University, it was different. You could choose to miss a meal. If you wanted, you could go to the dining-hall and watch others eat. You could eat as little or as much as you wished. You could also take some food out of the dining-hall to feed the birds or the fish. In the later years of the University, at the main campus, there was a man-made lake which contained some fish. Feeding those fish with bread from the dining-hall was one way in which the undergraduates relaxed after a hard day's work. Nobody would punish you if, for instance, you threw half a loaf, or even a whole loaf of bread into that lake for the fish. That was one of the ways of enjoying the independence of the young Republic of Zambia.

There was something else to write home about the University. There were no roll-calls and no out-of-bounds areas. You could get out into town and return to campus at any time. You could even sleep out of campus without any permission. Better still, you could smoke in public or even get thoroughly drunk. In fact, it was as if to be a legitimate university student, you had to get thoroughly drunk once in a while. That was the life of a university student. That was the life that Isaki was going to lead for the next seven years. And thereafter, he would graduate as a medical doctor.

There was academic freedom too. For the undergraduates, this turned out to mean the freedom to pass or fail. As roll-calls did not exist in the university, you could miss as many lectures as you wished without anybody showing any concern. The lecturers and professors minded their own business. In fact, most of them gave the impression that they had a lot of their own reading and writing to catch up with besides that lecturing business.

The lessons in the university were divided into lectures and tutorials. It was said that the former were optional whilst the latter were compulsory. Nonetheless, although attendance at tutorials was said to be obligatory, nobody would punish you if you decided to miss any of them. In fact, people did miss them for various reasons. A few lecturers might occasionally show concern by warning that those who missed tutorials could fail. But experience soon proved such lecturers wrong as quite a few people missed tutorials and still passed the exams.

Isaki wrote to Yosefe at the end of his first month at the University, describing what university life was like. He made sure to paint a wonderful picture of the institution as a way of encouraging Yosefe to work hard. To show how great being a university student was, he enclosed some cash in the letter. Isaki told his brother that that amount was only a fraction of the pocket money they had given him and that they would continue to give him throughout the seven years he was determined to spend in the university.

Yosefe loved receiving those letters for they gave him the rare opportunity to boast. That his elder brother was a university student was no small matter. Other boys at Chizongwe envied him. And it wasn't long before even teachers began to use him as an example in class.

'If you work hard,' they would tell the class, 'you too will go to the University of Zambia like Yosefe's brother.' And Yosefe would feel exalted and proud. But at times, his brother's success worked against him as some teachers tended to compare him with Isaki and not with his classmates. Even when he was top of the class, teachers were not impressed. For instance, if he scored seventy per cent in a test and was top of the class, they would rebuke him for not having done as well as Isaki used to.

'In a test like this, your brother used to score above eighty per cent. Why can't you do the same? Shame on you!' they would say. Feeling guilty and embarrassed, Yosefe would bow his head and suffer the humiliation silently and with pride.

TWENTY-TWO

For four years, Tisa and her children had not been in contact with members of Shuzi's family for fear of being struck by lightning. For the two sides to start talking, it was necessary that they went through a cleansing ceremony to nullify the effect of njazi. That cleansing could only take place if one of the parties, or a third party, suggested it.

In most cases, people not involved in the dispute were reluctant to propose a ceremony when the feuding people were still filled with mutual hatred. It was said that if a cleansing ceremony were rushed, the feuding parties might swear never to talk to each other again. The effects of a second declaration of njazi were more disastrous than those of the original one. In Nkhanza, nobody talked Shuzi and Tisa into the ceremony. It was Lwando who first suggested it. Concerned that the njazi had lasted so long, he paid headman Nkhanza a visit.

He went straight to his daughter's house and sent word to headman Nkhanza. Under normal circumstances, he would have reported his arrival to Shuzi. But because of the njazi, Lwando could not take risks. Njazi against his daughter was njazi against him too.

'Baba Nkhanza,' began Lwando, 'I travelled all the way from Mtendere to discuss a matter that has been worrying me for a long time. The njazi between my daughter and Baba Shuzi has been tormenting my heart. In the absence of father of Isaki, Baba Shuzi is the father to my grandchildren and husband to mother of Isaki. If he swears njazi, where will my grandchildren go for help? Why should they continue to live in this village if their guardian has disowned them?' Lwando asked and then paused. Headman Nkhanza said nothing.

'I came here not to destroy but to rebuild,' continued Lwando. 'Since the return to Walale of father of Isaki, a lot of things have been said and done which should not be. And things which ought to be done have not been done. For example, six years ago, my grandsons left this village in anger and appealed to me against Baba Shuzi. When Baba Shuzi came to Mtendere, he showed lack of interest in the matter and we sent him back to you with the request to give him men who could speak for him. Since then, we in Mtendere have been waiting. We want to resume those talks, but we cannot hold any discussions when we have njazi between those who are crucial in the matter,' said Lwando.

'Baba, those are words,' said headman Nkhanza. 'I cannot deny that we are guilty. We should have followed up the matter.'

'Now, the two sides affected by the njazi must drink the nthumo to nullify the njazi. I am here to request Baba Shuzi to go through the nthumo ritual with mother of Isaki. Once the two have reconciled and drunk the nthumo, we can sort out the other problems in the family,' said Lwando.

'That is overdue, baba,' said headman Nkhanza. 'I thank you for taking the initiative. I will pass on your request to Shuzi.'

'Talk to him whilst I am here. Where there are children, njazi must not be allowed to hang around for so long. Before I return to Mtendere, I want to know the response to my request. The rest of the preparations for the nthumo can come later.'

The following evening, headman Nkhanza gathered the elders to discuss the matter. The elders agreed that Lwando's proposal was good. They further agreed that the drinking of nthumo was long overdue. They consequently asked Shuzi for his reaction. Shuzi allowed a moment of silence to elapse before responding.

'Explain to my father-in-law that his proposal is good but that I am not ready for the nthumo because I am not sure that mother of Isaki will start obeying me. Tell him I do not want to bring calamities to the family by rushing the nthumo.'

That was a long night for headman Nkhanza. The message he had to take to Lwando was not the kind to take happily from a son-in-law to a father-in-law. But he had to take it all the same. His nduna accompanied him.

'Mother of Isaki,' said Lwando after he had been briefed by headman Nkhanza, 'do you hear those words?'

'I do, baba.'

'What have you to say?'

'What can I say? I have never been disobedient to my brother-in-law. If I had ever been, I would promise never to disobey him again. But as it is, I do not know what wrong I have done. The headman and the nduna can bear me witness. If I ever disobeyed him, why did he not report me to the headman or to you?'

'Obaba,' said Lwando, 'what mother of Isaki is telling you is that she is ready for the nthumo. She also assures you that your Shuzi has nothing to fear for she has never disobeyed him and has no intention of doing so. It is up to your man to make up his mind. Those are my words,' said Lwando.

'Indeed, baba, your words are words,' agreed headman Nkhanza. 'We only ask you to give us more time. The problem lies with our man. We are sorry that we have caused you so much trouble and that you have walked all the way from Mtendere in vain. We will see to it that our brother understands the urgency of the matter. As soon as we are ready, we will be in touch with you.'

Walking back to Mtendere, Lwando told himself that his trip had been worth it. Now that he had played his part, his only concern was that Tisa and his grandchildren would avoid making themselves vulnerable to the consequences of njazi. But when his wife heard of the outcome of his trip, she was not amused.

'Why did you not bring her and the children to our village? This is not a marriage. I have said this many times before,' said Mwaziona.

'It is not up to us to suggest a divorce. If they do not want our daughter, let them go to court,' Lwando insisted.

'But it is my daughter who is suffering. Is it not said that it is those that have stomach-ache who should open the door?'

'If you think that mother of Isaki is suffering, I suggest you go and hear from her own mouth what she thinks about the whole matter,' suggested Lwando.

'I am not going to a village where my daughter and grandchildren live under the threat of njazi. I will send for her so that I can talk to her in peace here.'

Tisa honoured her mother's invitation. Unlike her mother, she felt it was too late to give in.

'The worst is over,' said Tisa. 'Isaki is at the University and Yosefe in secondary school. Praise God, neither of them needs fees now that Kaunda has introduced free education. And Isaki works during the school holidays.

'I want to remain in Nkhanza until father of Isaki decides to divorce me in court. As a Christian, I will not initiate divorce. I draw my strength from the Word of God. My greatest strength comes from one Corinthians chapter seven, verses ten and eleven,' she told her parents, and recited the words of those two verses to them:

> *To the married I give this command (not I, but*
> *the Lord): A wife must not separate from her*
> *husband. But if she does, she must remain*
> *unmarried or else be reconciled to her husband.*
> *And a husband must not divorce his wife.*

'Do not worry about us,' Tisa continued. 'Njazi will not harm us for there is nothing that will compel us to speak to Baba Shuzi or even to walk into his compound. We live safely on our own. If Baba Shuzi does not like me, let him write to his brother and advise him to divorce me. Some years back, he threatened to do that. But Baba Shuzi has not succeeded. I do not want to assist him by taking the initiative.'

'Mwaziona, are those not words?' Lwando asked. 'You can see that it is Baba Shuzi who has stomach-ache and not us. Let him open the door if he so wishes. If he does not, it is he who will defecate inside his own house,' Lwando declared.

And they all laughed.

TWENTY-THREE

Fours years after entering the University of Zambia, Isaki was due to obtain his first degree. But that would not be the end. It would mark the beginning of his medical studies.

His medical school career was divided into three parts. He spent the first two years in the School of Natural Sciences. During his first year in that school, he followed four courses in Introductory Biology, Introductory Chemistry, Introductory Physics and Introductory Mathematics, all of which he had to pass before he could proceed to the second year of study. In his second year, he took four more courses. These were Biology of Cells and Systems, Plant and Animal Biology, Inorganic, Analytical and Physical Chemistry, and Organic Chemistry. He was required not only to pass all four courses but to pass them well in order to qualify for a place in the School of Medicine in his third year of study.

He worked hard and earned a place in the medical school. The first two years in the School of Medicine constituted the second part of his university studies. This was the period when he would follow what were referred to as pre-clinical courses. The courses he followed during the pre-clinical part included Anatomy, Biochemistry, Physiology, Pharmacology, Pathology, Microbiology and Psychology.

At the end of his pre-clinical studies, Isaki was among the first recipients of the B.Sc. (Human Biology) degree. Receiving the degree was, in itself, a great achievement. But that was not all which caused the excitement on that graduation day. Besides the fact that from that day, he would be able to put B.Sc. (Human Biology) against his name, an equally great achievement would be shaking hands with His Excellency Dr Kenneth David Kaunda, Chancellor of the University and President of the Republic of Zambia. How Isaki wished his father had attended his graduation!

Now that he had obtained the science degree, he could see

himself shaking hands with Kaunda again as he conferred upon Isaki the combined degrees of Bachelor of Medicine and Bachelor of Surgery within the next three years. Come that day, he would be able to add two more sets of letters against his name. Now he was Isaki Manda, B.Sc. In three years time, he would become Isaki Manda, B.Sc., M.B., B.S. On that day, his great dream would be completely realised. How he wished his father could attend at least his second graduation! That way, perhaps he would believe that education was indeed the key.

TWENTY-FOUR

V.V.'s farm was gradually being transformed. The changes that were taking place worried Musa. For a start, V.V. was no longer the baas that ıι had always known. He was fast losing some of his vital faculties. First to go was his sight. Later, his hearing also began to falter. Consequently, the misisi took more control of the affairs of the farm. Each time Musa asked to see V.V., she would offer to take the message. She would disappear into the house only to emerge shortly afterwards with a negative response.

V.V. Junior visited the farm more regularly. Musa hated that for V.V. Junior did not treat him the way his father did. He gradually stripped Musa of some of his responsibilities. The biggest blow came when he was told that he would no longer distribute the monthly rations. V.V. Junior would take personal charge of them. Worse still, he decided that during the distribution of rations, he would not require any assistance from Musa. Instead, V.V. Junior would be assisted by the store-keeper and the head-teacher of the farm school.

What further hurt Musa was that V.V. Junior did not give him reasons for that decision. But he was angered more as the workers suggested their own reasons why V.V. Junior was marginalising their once invincible foreman. Some said that their foreman was gradually losing his powers because he had not been back to Nchisi for consultations with his strong witch-doctors.

Others said that his first wife whom he banished to Northern Rhodesia had sought stronger muti to make him lose his job. Embittered by the rumours, Musa decided to find out why his authority was being diluted. He wanted to hear this directly from V.V. himself. But when he went to V.V.'s house and asked to see him, the misisi volunteered to take the message.

'No, you can't take the message. I would like to have a private discussion with him,' said Musa.

'Baas can't you see today,' she told him. 'If you can't let me take the message, you'll have to wait until he is in a position to meet you. He is not well at the moment.'

Two weeks later, Musa was back at V.V.'s house where V.V.'s wife saw him through the window. Without waiting for him to knock at the door, she went out to meet him.

'I'm afraid Baas is still too weak to get out of bed. Is it something that Junior cannot handle?' she enquired. 'Why don't you discuss the matter with him when he comes?'

When V.V. Junior came, he did not give Musa any opportunity to initiate the discussion. Upon learning from his mother that the foreman had something private to discuss with his father, V.V. Junior got onto his horse and rode straight to Musa's house.

'What do you want to discuss with Baas?' V.V. Junior asked.

'I wanted to speak to Baas about it but if you can give me an answer, I should be pleased. I am unhappy because some responsibilities are being taken away from me. I want to know what wrong I have done to deserve that punishment. I have served Baas well in many capacities for twenty-nine years.'

'Is that what has been worrying you, foreman? That is nothing to worry about. Indeed, you have done a lot for my father. But you're no longer as energetic as you used to be. Like my father, you need a rest. The duties of a foreman call for an energetic person who can reach every part of the farm daily. I don't think you are capable of that any longer.'

'But I'm still strong,' pleaded Musa.

'That's what you think, but those who see what you do are aware that you have lost the vigour which you had once upon a time. You cannot fight against nature. You and my father are both tired and deserve a rest. Besides, the world is changing. What was good for my father twenty-nine years ago is not all good today. That is why I'm giving some of your responsibilities to younger men who can march with the times. In the meantime, you'll continue to receive the same wages. Isn't that a fair deal?'

Musa shook his head to show his disappointment, but V.V. Junior was not moved. He got onto his horse and rode away.

A few months later, V.V. Junior quit teaching in order to give the affairs of the farm his total attention. Shortly after becoming a full-time farmer, V.V. Junior made further changes in the administration of the farm. He employed a young graduate of the University of Rhodesia as farm manager.

The employment of the farm manager affected Musa in a number of ways. Firstly, he had to vacate the three-bedroom house which he had occupied since his marriage to Rhoda. V.V. Junior told him to move back into the workers' compound. That set tongues wagging all over again. The farm workers said Musa was no longer foreman. Some said that he had been fired but that he was hanging around the farm because he had nowhere to go. This rumour did him a lot of harm when Rhoda began to believe it.

At first, Rhoda ignored it. But when women composed a song about it, she could no longer handle the situation. In the song, the women teased her for being proud despite the fact that her husband had lost his job. The song humiliated her considerably. She felt so embittered that each time she heard anyone sing it, she felt the urge to leap upon the person and rip her clothes to pieces. What added to Rhoda's frustration was the fact that her husband was behaving as though he did not hear the song. When she could no longer swallow it, she interrogated him.

'Baba,' she began, 'what do you think about the song that every woman is singing?'

'What song are you talking about?'

'You ask what song? Haven't you heard it? Every woman is singing it. Children are singing it. Why do you want to believe that all is still well?'

'What are you talking about, Rhoda? I tell you the truth, I haven't heard the song.'

'The truth is that you're no longer foreman here.'

'I'm still foreman, Rhoda. Yes, I have been relieved of some of my duties but I'm still foreman and I still get the wages of a foreman. Surely, that is what matters.'

'No! Money is not all that matters. Your name matters, baba. If all that counted was money, these women and children would not have composed a song about us. V.V. Junior doesn't want you here any more. He is taking your responsibilities away from you bit by bit in order to frustrate you so that you decide to quit. Are you going to wait here until he fires you?'

'What do you want me to do?'

'Find yourself another job. This is not the only farm. With your experience, any other farm would take you as foreman.'

'I'm not sure about that, Rhoda. Do you know of any farm without a foreman? I'll stay here until V.V. retires me. Nobody will fire me. His son cannot fire me because he is not the one who hired me. I have served his father faithfully for twenty-nine years. When his father feels I'm no longer needed, he will retire me with dignity.'

'So you want to be retired with dignity? Why don't you ask your V.V. for it? Why do you want to wait and subject me to all the insults from the labourers' wives?'

Musa bowed his head and pondered how he could respond to his wife's proposition.

For the first time in many months, the misisi allowed Musa to see V.V. When he told her what he wanted to talk to Baas about, she walked into the house and came out with him. He got the impression that Baas V.V., V.V. Junior and the misisi had already planned his retirement.

'Come to the office,' V.V. told him and he followed. There, he talked to him at length. V.V. took a long time because he spoke slowly and repeated himself quite often.

'Foreman, you and I are old now. For that reason, I'm glad that you have come to ask me to retire you. You've been a good foreman. Without you, I wouldn't have recruited so many people from your country. I thank you for that. Now, you deserve a rest. This is what I'll do for you. I'm going to give you one thousand pounds in traveller's cheques for your pension. In your country, that should last you many years. I'll also give you a driver and a lorry to take you to the Rhodesia-Zambia border. Once you're in your country, you should find your way home by public transport. Do you have any questions?'

'No, Baas.'

'Good. Now, you may start packing. As soon as you're ready, let me know,' V.V. told him and they shook hands.

Musa walked away with mixed feelings. He was relieved that he had done as Rhoda had instructed. But then, what next? He had no plans. After tormenting his heart as he walked to his house, he told himself that he had enough time to work things out. V.V. had not dictated to him when he should leave. It would be up to him to say when he was ready. In the meantime, he would discuss any further plans with Rhoda. After all, she had suggested that he ask V.V. to retire him with dignity. Now that he had done that with success, wouldn't she come up with another brilliant idea?

'V.V. has accepted my request for retirement,' he told her.

'Did you think he would object?' she asked. 'They decided to get rid of you a long time ago.'

'Rhoda, why do you say such things? I thought that was what you wanted me to do. I didn't want to ask V.V. to retire me. It was your idea. If you hadn't suggested it, I wouldn't have asked and if I hadn't asked, V.V. wouldn't have retired me.'

'What will you do now?' asked Rhoda after some silence.

'What do people do when they retire? We'll go home.'

'You want to return to Zambia? What will you do there?'

'We'll see what we can do. We could start a little business such as a grocery shop and a grinding mill.'

'No!' Rhoda protested. 'I have heard a lot about what people in your country do to those returning from here. They bewitch them, especially if they attempt to go into business. I don't want that to happen to me and my children.'

'What do you suggest, then?'

'Anything other than going back to your village. Can't you find a job in Lusaka or any other town in your country?'

'I could try that. But I would have to go alone first. Then after I find a suitable job and accommodation, I would return here for you and the children. In the meantime, you could go and live with my parents-in-law,' he told her.

'That's no problem. What matters is that you find another job. I could go to my parents with the girls, or I could go back to teaching.'

'Do you want to remain at the farm, then?'

'No!' said Rhoda emphatically. 'The labourers' wives would compose another song about me. I'm not going to bring further ridicule upon myself. If I have to go back to my teaching career, I'll try farm schools other than V.V.'s.'

TWENTY-FIVE

Isaki's second graduation was a big event for him. It was a big event for the University of Zambia and it was an equally big event for the Republic of Zambia as a whole. In December 1972, the first batch of medical students had completed all the requirements for the award of the joint degree of Bachelor of Medicine and Bachelor of Surgery. Isaki was one of them.

His Excellency Dr Kenneth David Kaunda, Chancellor of the University, was going to confer the degrees upon them. Like most of his fellow graduands, Isaki wanted his parents to witness his graduation. Three years earlier when he received his B.Sc. (Human Biology) degree, Isaki regretted that his parents had not attended. He had wished his father had been there so that he could see how education was the key, just as Chief Sairi the Third used to tell them during Isaki's primary school days back in the mid-fifties. But he had lost contact with his father. Now, three years later, he still didn't have any contact with him.

This time, however, Isaki had taken precautions to ensure that his mother witnessed his graduation. After completing his studies, he took up employment as a general practitioner at the Kitwe General Hospital. Two weeks before the graduation day, he travelled to Nkhanza village and fetched his mother. He did not want her to miss the big day. He wanted her to watch with her own eyes as her son shook hands with Kaunda. His mother was not the only family member who witnessed his graduation. His younger brother Yosefe was there too. He was then a second-year student of Law, having joined the University the previous academic year.

The campus was flamboyant on that great day as academic staff, graduands and former graduates of the University walked about in their academic gowns. Tisa marvelled at all the fuss. She knew that her son had not stayed in school so long for nothing. But it had never occurred to her that in the end he would be part of a national attraction. She had never seen men wearing robes and funny caps before. Now, here was her own son as part and parcel of the spectacle.

She was to see more. Isaki had not told her that Kaunda would be there. He had concealed that fact from her in order to give her a pleasant surprise. She had never seen Kaunda in person. So far, she had only seen his image on her membership card of the United National Independence Party and on some posters. When he arrived, Kaunda was also in an attractive gown. It was the only one of its kind on the scene.

'That's Kaunda!' exclaimed Tisa to Yosefe who sat next to her at the graduation forum.

'Yes, it is,' said Yosefe.

'He is coming to a address a rally here?'

'No. He too has come for the graduation.'

'So this thing is important,' she remarked.

As the conferring of the degrees progressed, Tisa noticed that Kaunda personally shook hands with each graduand. As candidate after candidate received their scrolls, their fathers and mothers would leap up from the crowd and rush for their graduating child in total jubilation. Their mothers would ululate and dance towards the dais where Kaunda stood as he waited for the next graduand's name to be called.

Tisa was atypical in that regard. When Isaki's turn came, she remained motionless. She did not jump to her feet like other parents before her had done. She did not ululate and dance like a drunken woman either. Seeing other mothers and fathers share their joy and pride in the success of their children made her conscious of the fact that she had been without a husband for so many years. She wondered how she had managed to educate her son to the extent that he had become one of the most learned people in Zambia.

Tisa felt so sorry for herself that rather than run drunkenly to meet her son after he had received his degree, she walked to him slowly and shook hands with him. Thereafter, she went back to her seat, bowed her head and said a short prayer. She thanked the Lord for having enabled her to educate her child. She prayed that Isaki should henceforth look after her and his three younger brothers and one younger sister. When she completed her prayer, she wept.

'I wish your father were here to see all this for himself,' she told her sons when the graduation ceremony was over.

'I feel the same, mother,' said Isaki.

'I don't,' Yosefe told them but neither his elder brother nor his mother paid any attention to his comment.

TWENTY-SIX

Musa was driven to the Rhodesia-Zambia border in a lorry which V.V. provided. According to V.V., after crossing the border Musa was to find his own way home. But Musa had his own plan. He had to abide by the pact he made with Rhoda. He would not proceed to his home district for he had no intention of retiring from full-time employment. He wasn't an old man. He was going to stop over in Lusaka and look for a job.

Before leaving for Lusaka, he took Rhoda and their two daughters to her parents. He would not let her go on her own. That would appear as if he were abandoning her for ever. He wouldn't abandon Rhoda. She was still so young and attractive that she would easily find another man if he showed any signs of abandoning her. If she fell in love with another man, he would go crazy. He wanted to explain his plans to his father-in-law. He had to know that Musa was leaving her behind only temporarily.

His parents-in-law appreciated his plans. It was a foolish man who took his wife and children with him before he was sure where he was going. His parents-in-law assured him that his family would be safe with them. In turn, he told them that he would be in touch with his wife as soon as he found a good job in Zambia.

'Baba, I would like to request you to keep our belongings till I come for my family,' said Musa. 'These include beds, bedding, a dining table, dining chairs and kitchen utensils. There are also three bicycles and three sewing-machines. Please keep two bicycles and two sewing-machines safely for me. The third bicycle is yours and the third sewing-machine is for my mother-in-law.'

As he bid them farewell, he gave his father-in-law one hundred pounds and his wife two hundred.

Although he had never lived in Lusaka, Musa was not worried about what he would do once he was there. The town was not entirely new to him as he had passed through there each time he travelled to Fort Jameson. In addition, he had heard from those who had been there on job hunts that the best thing for a stranger to do was to report to the nearest council office.

His baggage comprised two trunks and a wooden box. One trunk contained his clothing and the other blankets whereas the wooden box carried an assortment of kitchenware.

He arrived in Lusaka by train before six in the morning. His first task was to go to the nearest council office, but he wondered how he would walk around in search of the council offices with two trunks and a wooden box. However, upon enquiries, the guards at the railway station told him he could leave his baggage at the station storeroom. He would not be charged anything during the first forty-eight hours.

The city council offices were within walking distance from the railway station. When he enquired from the station guards what sort of assistance he would expect to get from the council, their response shocked him. They told him that without certificates, he could not get a good job. After further enquiries, he was advised to approach the city council personnel department.

At the city council, the first person he asked about jobs directed him to the reception where he found a middle-aged man and a teenage girl. The man had a pen in his right hand and a big book in front of him, whilst the girl was holding a telephone receiver and talking into the mouthpiece.

'Can we help you?' the man asked him in English.

'I don't understand that,' said Musa in a variety of Nyanja which betrayed his Rhodesian exposure.

The man smiled and repeated the question in Nyanja.

'I want a job,' said Musa.

The man looked at the girl beside him and the two of them smiled at each other.

'Didn't you hear what I said?' asked Musa.

The man looked him straight in the face and then, without uttering a word, pointed out to him a multitude of men who were struggling for anterior positions in a queue.

'If you want work, join that queue,' he was told.

'What sort of work are they queuing for?'

'Any. Digging drains; felling trees; slashing grass; sweeping the streets or markets or bus stations; cleaning public toilets – those kind of jobs.'

'Is that all you have?'

'What kind do you want? If you want an office job, you must write an application letter.'

'I should write a letter for a job?'

'Yes. And in English.'

'I can't write English but I have a lot of experience in farm work. I was a foreman at a big tobacco farm in Rhodesia,' he said with pride. The girl on the telephone smiled and the man with a big book in front of him laughed.

'There's no such work here,' the girl told him. 'Try the labour office.'

'How do I get there?'

'Take a taxi. Any taxi driver should know where the labour office is,' said the man.

The taxi driver stopped at an ancient-looking building and told him, 'This is the labour office.' Musa gave him a one-kwacha note and walked towards the building. There were many people all around the building. He wanted to find the entrance but that proved impossible. There were boys here and boys there.

Unlike at the council offices, there was no queue here and no order. All he could see were pockets of boys jostling each other and shouting at the top of their voices. His first hurdle was to find out what those boys were fighting for. He wanted to see who was at the centre of each heap of people. But that alone was no easy task as the boys who surrounded the poor fellow kept on jumping up and down like people competing for height. All he could do eventually was enquire from those near him what was happening.

'They are fighting for numbers,' they told him.

'What numbers?'

'Are you here for the first time?' asked one.

'I'm new in this country,' said Musa. 'I arrived this morning from Walale,' he added.

Those who heard him eyed him with a mixture of ridicule and sympathy.

'This is the labour office, big man,' one told him. 'We're here for work. But first we have to be given a number. Then, each morning, for the whole of this week, everyone who has a number has to come here to find out if his number has come out. The numbers for each day will be called out every morning at seven. If your number is called out, you know there is a job for you.'

'What kind of job?'

'Any. Felling trees; digging trenches; cutting grass; gardening; sweeping markets and bus stations; emptying dustbins; cleaning public toilets, and so on. Are you looking for a job?'

'Yes.'

'Then, you better try your luck for a number over there,' the young man told him, pointing to one of the pockets where crowds of youths were fighting for numbers.

He considered that piece of advice and decided that it was in bad taste. What would Rhoda think of him if he accepted such menial jobs? If those were the only jobs on offer, then it was not the right place for him. He had to leave immediately. Besides, he was tired, sleepy and hungry.

'Any luck?' one of the railway guards asked him.

'None,' said Musa. 'I went to the city council and then to the labour office. They know nothing about farm foremen.'

'You reached the labour office?'

'Yes. Someone at the council suggested that I try there. You know what I found? There were crowds of good-for-nothing boys fighting for numbers. What a waste of youthful energy! Those young men would make excellent farm workers where I have come from,' he lamented.

'What do you intend to do now?' asked one of the guards.

'I'm hungry and tired. Where can I find a rest house?'

'First you need some food, don't you? There is a restaurant at the station. The food is good and inexpensive. You can eat there. Thereafter, you may take a taxi to the Stanley Hotel. It is the least expensive in town.'

'And my baggage?'
'It will be safe here.'

He slept soundly that night, but awoke early in the morning and began to toss about in bed. Since Lusaka did not have any work for him, he would move on to a Copperbelt town. Perhaps he could get a job in the mines. Or better still, there could be a farm which needed an experienced foreman.

He took the evening train for Kitwe which arrived at six the following morning. As in Lusaka, the station guards said they would keep his baggage free of charge for forty-eight hours.

He had heard that the mines usually had an assortment of jobs. With his experience as a foreman, they should be able to find him a supervisory position. After enquiries, he was directed to a personnel officer who asked him a few questions. His answers to three of those questions did him some damage.

'Have you ever worked underground?'

'No.'

'What is your educational qualification?'

'I never went to school.'

'How old are you now?'

'Fifty.'

'You're fifty?'

'Yes.'

'I'm sorry, we've no jobs for fifty-year-old men. If you were a little younger, we could have tried you as a watchman.'

'I don't want to be a watchman.'

'What job do you have in mind?'

'I want the kind of job I'm used to. I've just returned from Walale where I was a farm foreman. If you have a department where you require a foreman, I'm the right man.'

'We don't. Try elsewhere,' the personnel officer told him, stood up and extended his right hand for a farewell handshake. 'Have a good day,' he added as they shook hands.

Musa was frustrated. The mining company had many jobs. The young man in that office didn't like him, but he would not give up. He would come back and sit in his office until he offered him a job. But first, he needed to eat something and take a rest.

The following day, he was back at the personnel office after spending a night at some no-star hotel in the town.

'Young man, I'm back,' he told the personnel officer. 'Find me a job. Anything that would suit a man like me.'

'As I told you yesterday, the company has no jobs for people of your age. Here, we need energetic young men who can use pickaxes and hoes underground.'

'Please, give me a chance. I have a wife and two daughters to look after,' Musa pleaded.

'Where are they?'

'I left them in Rhodesia. As soon as I find employment, I'll send them transport money so that they may join me here.'

The personnel officer considered his plea for a while.

'See me tomorrow afternoon,' he told him.

On his third day in Kitwe, Musa was employed by the mining company and was given a one-bedroom house with electricity. The toilets and bathrooms were communal ones.

He was assigned to the mine market where he would double as a collector of the daily rental from the marketeers as well as a cleaning supervisor. There were no people employed as cleaners for the market. The marketeers themselves were responsible for cleaning the place every day between five and six in the evening before they left the premises.

At first, the job seemed manageable. But it did not take long before Musa discovered that his status was actually that of an unskilled labourer, for there were some parts of the market which the marketeers did not clean. These included the toilets and shower rooms. Nobody had told him that he would be responsible for cleaning these. He first learnt of it from a health inspector who visited the market twice a week. When the health inspector told him, Musa was shocked. Rhoda would not want him to keep such a degrading job. And then there was the question of accommodation. Rhoda would not want to share communal toilets and showers. He would have to ask for a better house.

Not knowing to whom to address his housing problem, he decided to approach the personnel officer who recruited him. That way, he could present him with two problems at the same time. Later, he wished that personnel officer had referred him to someone else. His response made Musa suspect that there was something that the young officer did not understand about him.

'Can I help you?' the personnel officer asked him.

'I've come here for two things. Firstly, that job you gave me at the market. Do I have to clean the toilets and the showers?'

'Your duty is to ensure that the entire place is clean every day. That includes the toilets and showers.'

'I can't clean toilets. I have never done it in my whole life. I told you that in Rhodesia, I was a farm foreman and not a cleaner of anything, let alone of communal toilets. You'll have to find someone else to do that.'

'And what's your other complaint?'

'The house. Firstly, it is too small. I need a three-bedroom house for I have a wife and two daughters aged twelve and fourteen. They'll be joining me soon. Secondly, I don't like sharing toilets and shower rooms. I've never shared these before. Where I've come from, I had a three-bedroom house with electricity and its own toilet and bathroom.'

'Do you have any other complaint?'

'That's all for the time being.'

'Your complaints are too difficult for me to handle. I don't want to tell you any lies. The company will not employ two people at that market. One person is adequate for that job. If you don't like it, you're free to leave. As for the house, people of your qualifications can only be accommodated in the location where you are at the moment. If you don't like the house, I suggest that you find your own accommodation in town and pay the rent. That's company policy. I'm aware that the company intends to demolish all those one-bedroom structures and construct better houses in their place. But until that is done, people like you will have to put up with the inconvenience.'

'You don't want to help me, do you?'

'It is not up to me. I'm only telling you company policy. If I were you, I would take what is on offer,' the personnel officer advised him. 'You may not find a better job.'

Musa was speechless. He walked out of the office and headed straight for his one-bedroom structure. That night, he could not find much sleep. If what the personnel officer had told him was true, what would he do? He was not going to continue working as a cleaner of toilets! But if he turned down the job altogether, what would he do next? Return to Rhodesia and join Rhoda, or proceed to Chipata where he would become a mere villager?

He could go back to Rhodesia. That could be good for he was missing Rhoda and his daughters. They too must be missing him. He could go back there and tell Rhoda that he did not like the job he had found. Or he could tell her that he did not like the entire country. She would appreciate his position.

But then, how would he earn his living? If the only baas for whom he had worked for twenty-nine years said his services were no longer required, how would a white man to whom he was a total stranger offer him any employment? Rhoda might appreciate the fact that he did not like his motherland any longer, but she would not agree to look after an unemployed husband. She had married a foreman and did not see herself suddenly becoming the wife of a loafer.

He would not return to Rhodesia. But if he did not get a better job, he was not going to remain in town indefinitely. He did not want to continue doing a dirty job. He had an image to protect. In the end, he would have to find means of earning a living. Perhaps he could return to his home town. It would be interesting to experience the difference between the town of Fort Jameson which he left several years ago and the new town of Chipata. The problem there was that he would have to survive by tilling the land. He would need land.

But land would not be his only problem if he chose to return to Nkhanza village. There would be Tisa to face after so long. Where would she be living at that moment? Where were his children, particularly his sons?

If Tisa were still in Nkhanza, he would not have settling-in problems for he could move into her house. He also wouldn't have to look for a fresh piece of land. He could join her and work with her.

But would she accept him back? His return to Nkhanza would depend on Tisa's situation and attitude towards him. He would have to find out if she was still in Nkhanza or not. He was going to write to her that evening. He would also write to Rhoda and explain the situation. He would tell both Tisa and Rhoda what his circumstances were and leave it up to each one of them to decide what to say to him in response. If Rhoda told him to stop cleaning toilets and return to Rhodesia, he would do as she said. With some luck, she might tell him that she was going to use whatever influence she had to get him a job.

House No. XY, Section R, Wusakile, Kitwe.
31-10-73

Dear mother of Isaki,

How are you and the children? I am writing this letter only to inform you that I am back in Zambia. I left Rhodesia because V.V. retired me. I currently have a job in the mining company here in Kitwe. It is not a good job. I work at a market where I am expected to make the marketeers clean up the place at the end of each day.

What makes the job particularly difficult is that the marketeers are mostly women. They are difficult women. There are places within the market which none of them want to clean. These include the communal toilets. Sometimes I have to do the cleaning myself, which is not a pleasant thing to do.

Something else that I find intolerable is that I am alone. I left Rhoda and the children with her parents because I did not want to be travelling with them as I went from one town to another in search of employment.

Please answer my letter so that I may know how you are getting on with the children.

I am your husband of all times,
Musandivute

After completing the letter to Tisa, he wrote one to Rhoda.

House No. XY, Section R, Wusakile, Kitwe, Zambia.

31-10-73

Dear Rhoda,

How are you and the children? I am writing this letter from Kitwe, a mining town. I have not found a job yet. At the moment, I have temporary work at a mine market but I don't like it. I am responsible for the cleanliness of the place. I have to make the marketeers clean up at the end of each day. But sometimes I have to do some cleaning too.

I am still trying to get a better job. This one is no good because they don't provide good housing. I live in a one-bedroom house which has neither bathroom nor toilet. I have to share communal toilets and showers with two other families.

Please answer this letter so that I may know how you are getting on. Have you found a job yet? If so, where? Is there any possibility that I could also find a job there? Please greet my parents-in-law and the girls.

I am your husband of all times,
Musandivute.

TWENTY-SEVEN

Tisa received her husband's letter with feelings of some relief, great disappointment and a bit of pity. Although she was glad to hear from him after a long time, she was disappointed that he had thought of her only after he was no longer foreman. She wondered why he was all on his own. Could it be that Rhoda had abandoned him now that he was no longer important? And the contents of his letter did not impress her. Other than saying where he was and what he was doing, he did not explain why he had not written for so long. Nor did he make any reference to his many unfulfilled promises.

In spite of her disappointment, Tisa felt some degree of pity for her husband. The foreman Musa she knew was a man with considerable vanity. He would not sink so low as to work at a market. She could not imagine him spending a whole day quarrelling with women who refused to sweep the filth they had created. The foreman Musa she knew was incapable of cleaning even his own teacup. She could not see how he might be expected to clean communal toilets, of all places. She was certain he would do that only under pressure. If that was all the work that he could get, she wondered why he did not return home. Tilling the land was a more respectable occupation.

She wished she could discuss his predicament with Shuzi. Perhaps they could convince Musa to come back home. But she was not talking to Shuzi since they were under the threat of njazi. Despite that, she wanted him to know that his brother was back in Zambia. She would inform him through the headman. She would also send Isaki the letter from his father. Since he too was in Kitwe, he could look his father up and take him to his house.

Isaki would not let his father suffer.

Musa was about to prepare his lunch when he saw a car arrive at his one-bedroom residence in Wusakile Mine Compound. That was a surprise for he did not know anybody in the town. As the car parked, he went out of the house to see who the visitor was. The young man who emerged from the car walked steadily towards Musa. And he slowly moved towards his visitor, studying him from foot to head. When they met, the two eyed each other all over again.

'My son!' exclaimed Musa.

'And you must be my father,' his visitor responded, offering his right hand. And they shook hands.

'Who are you?' asked Musa. 'Isaki or Yosefe?'

'Isaki.'

'You're a man,' said Musa. 'How did you know I was here?'

'My mother told me. I received a letter from her this morning. How are you, baba?'

'Please come in. This is where I live,' he told him. 'Sit on the floor. There are neither beds nor chairs in this house. Where are you at the moment?'

'Right here in Kitwe.'

'What do you do? Good jobs are rare in this country. When I arrived, I first tried to look for a job in Lusaka. Nobody could offer me any. When I moved here, the only job they could give me is that of supervising the marketeers who clean the mine market. I hate the job.'

'I heard all that from my mother. You were lucky to get the job that you say you don't like. Many people are unemployed.'

'And yourself? What job do you do and how did you get it?'

'These days, education matters a lot.'

'That's what everyone has been telling me since my arrival in this country. What's all this talk about education?'

'Employers require people with some certificate. As for me, I spent seven years at the University of Zambia where I studied medicine. I'm a doctor at the Kitwe General Hospital.'

'You went as far as university?'

'Yes. I have three degrees. Father, education is the key to one's future. I'll never forget those words from Chief Sairi the Third way back in 1956 at Sairi Lower Primary School.'

'Who paid for your education?'

'My mother,' Isaki told his father.

'And Yosefe? Where is he?'

'He is studying law at the University of Zambia. This is his third year. Soon, we'll have a lawyer in the family.'

'Who has been paying for his education?'

'Until recently, our mother has been paying. But now that I'm working, I've taken full responsibility,' said Isaki. 'Well, father, let me say what I came for. I came to take you home. My mother doesn't want you to be here on your own. She doesn't want you to suffer. She wants you back home.'

'Your mother sent you?'

'Yes. And I agree with her. This place is no good for you. There's no reason why you should suffer like someone who has no home. I must take you back to the village.'

'When?'

'Right now, I have to take you to my house. And a week before Christmas, we'll travel to Chipata by bus,' said Isaki.

'What about my work?'

'That is no work, father. I'll take you to the personnel office and tell them to release you with immediate effect. At your age, you need to rest. They are exploiting you.'

Musa agreed with his son. The job was not good for him. He had to go back to Nkhanza with him. Of course, he still wished he could go back to Rhodesia to join Rhoda but she had not replied to his letter. All he could do now was to go back to his village, and from there, contact Rhoda again.

But how would he be received in Nkhanza? Was Tisa anxiously awaiting his return so that she could take revenge for his having abandoned her in that village for seventeen years? And he wondered what the entire village thought of him. Wouldn't the men say of him that he was not quite a man? And the women? Wouldn't they be eager to compose humiliating songs about him?

'I want to come to Nkhanza with you but then, I'm afraid of a few things,' Musa told his son. 'Will your mother welcome me?'

'My mother will be angry with me if I don't take you home.'

'And the headman?'

'Father, have no fear. You'll be welcomed by everyone in the village. The only problem I foresee is in connection with your brother, Baba Shuzi.'

'What about him?'

'He is not talking to any member of our family. So, don't expect him to come to my mother's house to greet you. He and his entire family don't come into my mother's compound and none of us go into his.'

'Why is that so?'

'It happened over four years ago. Baba Shuzi swore by njazi that any member of our family who crossed into his compound should be struck dead by lightning and those from his compound who crossed into ours should be met by the same doom. Since then, we have not been on talking terms.'

'That is bad.'

'It is. But don't let it bother you. I believe things will now come back to normal. First, however, you must return home. The rest will be taken care of,' Isaki advised his father.

TWENTY-EIGHT

After sunrise, the bus stopped at Katawa and Musa and his son alighted. They had travelled all night from Lusaka, having left Kitwe by the same bus at ten in the morning the previous day.

As they entered the village, Musa was ashamed of himself for his only baggage was a suitcase that his son was carrying. How could he make everyone aware that he had two trunks and one wooden box in Kitwe at his son's home? He wished he could announce to them all that the suitcase they were seeing was not all he had. He wished he could let them know that in addition to the two trunks and one wooden box that he had left in Kitwe, he had also left with his wife Rhoda in Rhodesia some beds, a lot of blankets, an expensive dining table, several chairs, an assortment of brand new kitchen utensils, three bicycles and three sewing-machines. He wished he could tell them that the suitcase they were seeing had been given to him by his son only for clothes that he would require before his trunks and wooden box arrived. So Musa did not enter Nkhanza village with the triumph befitting a man who had been away in Walale for many years. He looked like one who had been beaten by heavy rains.

Tisa was seated outside her kitchen. A short distance away, Shuzi was sharpening an axe. Isaki led his father to his mother's house. He had to ensure that he did not put his father in a situation where he would be tempted to talk to his brother. That could be disastrous for the family. Although Musa was not in the village when his brother pronounced njazi, he was affected.

Unlike his previous arrivals, this one was marked by total silence. There was an air of solemnity everywhere. His wife stood up, walked towards her son and relieved him of the suitcase. After depositing it in the house, she re-emerged to offer her husband a stool. Thereafter, she brought out a reed mat and laid it next to where she had seated her husband. Isaki found himself a log and made himself as comfortable as he could. When they were all seated, Tisa rose from her reed mat, tiptoed to her husband, knelt before him and offered him her right hand.

'How was your journey?'

'It was alright. Thank you.'

'And how were the children when you left Walale?'

'I left them and their mother with their grandparents. I hope they will be alright there in the meantime,' he told her. Tisa then rose from her knees and moved back to her reed mat. After sitting silently beside her husband for some time, she rose and called out to her youngest sons, Luka and Davide, and introduced them to their father.

'These children are now all men,' remarked Musa.

'You have been away a long time, baba. When you left us here, Davide was only a baby,' Tisa reminded him.

'How old are you?' he asked the younger of the two.

'Nearly nineteen,' said Davide.

More silence befell them. Later, Tisa got up from her reed mat and instructed her two youngest sons to catch a cock which she was going to prepare for her husband's meal. After issuing that instruction, she left for the kitchen. Isaki also excused himself and told his father he was going to inform headman Nkhanza about their arrival. Left alone, Musa began to doze on his stool. Fearing that he might fall off the stool, he got up and followed his wife into the kitchen.

'Please, Tisa, I need to lie down,' he pleaded. 'I was dozing on the stool.'

'You must be tired,' she said and went into the house to prepare a place for him to sleep. When she had done that, she invited him in. She had prepared a reed mat for him.

'Is this where I will rest?' he asked. 'Is there no bed?'

'I have been sleeping on this hard floor for the past seventeen years,' she told him.

'Is it not uncomfortable?'

'It is not hard for me. With time, you too will get used to it,' she reassured him and then left him alone.

Whilst Musa rested, Isaki and headman Nkhanza discussed Shuzi. Musa and his brother could not greet each other. It had now become necessary that the two families drink the nthumo.

The headman decided to talk to Tisa and Shuzi separately. He had to persuade them to agree to drink the nthumo. But Isaki told him that he did not want to have anything to do with the nthumo because he did not initiate the njazi. His task had been to bring his father home and now, he had to get back to his job.

Headman Nkhanza shook his head several times in despair. He did not know what to say to the young man. Indeed, was it not the grown-ups who had erred? But he could not tell exactly who amongst them was to blame. Was it Tisa? Could it be said with all sincerity that she had not behaved in a manner expected of a well brought up Ngoni woman? A woman who had not been properly trained by her parents would not have remained in her husband's village for so many years despite her husband's manifest negligence of his responsibilities. If mother of Isaki were not a properly brought up woman, she would have left Nkhanza for her parental village the day Shuzi pronounced njazi. She didn't. It would not be easy to apportion blame against her.

Or could one blame Shuzi? Would it be correct to say that he had failed to look after his brother's wife and children? He was responsible for the njazi that stood between him and mother of Isaki, but would he have gone to that extent if his brother had been in constant touch with him? Perhaps, if anybody was to take the blame for the misunderstanding between Shuzi and mother of Isaki, it had to be Baba Musandivute. But of what could one accuse him? He was not the first man to leave his wife and children in the custody of his brother.

Maybe he, as headman, was to blame for not having sorted out the njazi on time. But nthumo could only be administered if all the parties concerned were agreeable. He had done what was required but Shuzi had made any reconciliation difficult.

He did not have answers to those questions. But did it matter whether he had answers or not? What was crucial was to get Shuzi and mother of Isaki to drink the nthumo. Any other issues could wait.

He took his nduna with him. They started from Tisa's house where they first welcomed Musa back home. Thereafter, they briefly narrated to him how his brother declared njazi.

'We felt it was necessary to explain this to you lest you be surprised why your brother is not coming to greet you,' headman Nkhanza told him.

'Njazi is not something that people choose to play with. It kills. Our mission now is to request your wife and your brother to agree to drink the nthumo. If they don't, you will not be able to talk to your brother.'

'Obaba' began Musa, 'you mean to tell me that my wife and my brother have been under the threat of njazi all these years and nobody persuaded them to drink the nthumo? Why did you leave it for so long? And what makes you think of it now? Is it because I am here?'

'We tried, but your brother refused. And there was nothing we could do. Yes, we decided to give the matter another chance when we heard that you were back from Walale. We do not want you to be unable to talk to your own brother.'

'Obaba, I thank you for your efforts,' Musa told them. 'I thank you with all my heart for having kept my wife in this village for so long in spite of her problems with my brother. But about this nthumo business, I do not think you should bother yourselves. Since my brother refused to co-operate the last time it was suggested, I do not think you should plead with him again. Tell him that I do not want to talk to him. Let us continue with the njazi. I want you to tell him something else. I want to take all my cattle out of his kraal. I will build my own. Those are my words.'

'Those are not words, baba,' said headman Nkhanza. 'A man must never part with his own brother for whatever reason. If you want to have separate kraals, that is alright but it must not be on account of a quarrel between you. Allow us to request Shuzi to drink the nthumo with mother of Isaki.'

'Why was that not done before I came? Now that I am back, people want to do things to please me. I am not interested in that nthumo affair. Tell Shuzi that all I want are my cattle. Once he has separated my cattle from his, I will not want to have anything else to do with him.'

'Baba, those are harsh words,' the nduna told him. 'Do you not know that we are experiencing these problems because of you?'

'You want to blame me for this? If I were here, this would not have happened.'

'That is what the nduna is saying,' said headman Nkhanza. 'If you had not left your wife and children in this village for so many years, we would not be arguing like this. But this is not the time for blaming each other. We are here to end all squabbles. We have told you what we want to do and now, we will proceed to your brother and tell him the same.'

Headman Nkhanza rose and signalled to his nduna to follow. As the two men walked towards Shuzi's compound, Tisa, who had been following the discussion from her kitchen, clapped her hands once.

'Men!' she said, and continued with her cooking.

Shuzi was expecting them. He did not like the fact that he could not talk to his brother on account of the njazi that existed between him and his brother's wife. He disliked his sister-in-law more than he had ever done before. Why had she instructed her son to take his father directly to her house? Isaki should have brought his father to him first. And why had the headman and his nduna spent so much time at Tisa's house? What kind of medicine did the woman have to command so much authority over men? He was not going to succumb to that charm of hers. He was not so weak as to give in to a woman.

'Your brother is back from Walale,' the headman began.

'I know that,' said Shuzi.

'Do not hold my tongue,' said headman Nkhanza. 'We are here to help you. Now that your brother is here, it is essential that you and mother of Isaki drink the nthumo. The last time this was suggested by Baba Lwando, it was you who made things difficult. We left you alone then. But this time, you have no choice. If you want to talk to your brother, you must agree to go through the nthumo drinking ritual with your sister-in-law. We have come to ask you to give us an assurance that you will go through that ritual. Once you give us an affirmative response, I will arrange for a witch-doctor to come and administer the nthumo.'

'You say that last time I made things difficult. I disagree. What

I said then was that I was willing to drink the nthumo on condition that mother of Isaki, and the two boys she had poisoned against me, were prepared to apologise for their unbecoming behaviour. I further wanted an assurance from them that they would not repeat that kind of behaviour. That was all I asked. Did your Tisa do that? No! She remained as hard as a witch. And you let her get away with it. Do you see the result of that now? She is still sowing seeds of hatred in this family.'

'In which way?' the nduna asked.

'Look at what happened this morning. Yes, there is njazi between Tisa and I. But should that stop my brother from coming to my house? I have not been able to greet my brother all this time only because your Tisa connived with that spoilt son of hers to take him directly to her house. Njazi against me is njazi against him too. For that reason, he should not have gone to Tisa's house. He should have come to me. I was supposed to keep him in my compound until such time that we all drank the nthumo. Do you see how she has compounded the problem now?'

'She has not compounded anything,' said headman Nkhanza.

'Baba! Why do you say such things? That woman is all out to make this family suffer. She poisoned our sons and now she wants to poison my own brother too. Do you condone that?'

'Shuzi, listen to me. Mother of Isaki has not done anything so far. If you did not want your brother to go to his wife's house, why did you not fetch him where he was going to die like a man who had no relative? Tisa sent her son to bring his father home. You must be grateful to her for that.

'I do not condone any destructive behaviour. I always want to encourage a spirit of co-operation and constructiveness. I commend mother of Isaki. But I do so only because she has demonstrated clearly that she believes in building and not destroying this village. If she were destructive, she would not have remained in this village all these years that her husband has been away. You should thank her for that.'

'Thank her? Not me!'

'Baba Shuzi, you do not know what you are talking about,' the nduna told him. 'As headman Nkhanza has told you, we are here to help you. Tell us one thing. Do you or do you not agree to drink the nthumo with your sister-in-law?'

'Those are words,' the headman concurred. 'Tell us what we should say to your brother.'

'What I want to tell my brother cannot be conveyed through emissaries. Tell him that I would like to discuss many things with him.'

'And where and when would you like to do that?' headman Nkhanza asked him.

'Here and now.'

'You would like him to come here?'

'Yes.'

'Well, Baba Nduna, take that message to Baba Musandivute while I wait here,' said headman Nkhanza.

'Do you want me to do that, Baba Shuzi?' the nduna asked.

'Of course. As for the nthumo, tell him that I would like to receive an apology from Tisa before I can drink it with her.'

'I will take the message,' the nduna said and walked across to where Musa was seated. The headman believed that Musa's response would give him and the nduna more power with which to negotiate with Shuzi. After a little while, Musa rose and walked towards them. Then, at some point between his brother's compound and his wife's, he stopped and called out to Shuzi.

'Shuzi, listen carefully,' he began. 'I am still tired after my long journey. I do not want to stand here and quarrel with you for long. While I was away, you drew a boundary between my wife's compound and yours, and declared njazi between my wife and children and yourself and your wives and children. By pronouncing njazi against my wife and children, you declared njazi against me too. For that reason, I do not want to talk to you. Remain there with your wives and children and I will remain here in peace with my wife and children.

'That is all I have to tell you. Do not expect to hear from me any more. You caused this to happen between us. So, you must pay for it,' Musa concluded and walked back to his stool majestically.

The nduna walked back to Shuzi's compound, smiling.

'What did I tell you? That woman has poisoned my brother against me,' lamented Shuzi.

'No, you are wrong, Shuzi. Mother of Isaki is not poisoning anybody. The problem is that there is njazi between your family and your brother's. If this njazi is neutralised, all these misunderstandings will cease. That is why we came to you. We have said all that there is to be said. We will leave you to consider our plea. Once you have decided to drink the nthumo, you may let me know and I will seek a reputable witch-doctor for that purpose,' headman Nkhanza told him. After that, he rose to leave, and his nduna followed.

TWENTY-NINE

For a whole week, Musa and his brother would not talk to each other. Tisa had decided to give them a week in which to reconcile. After that, she would intervene. Before he left for his duties in Kitwe, Isaki told her that he would support any action she took regarding the njazi and nthumo issue. But he reiterated his stand. He did not want to be involved any further in any problem regarding his father. Having brought him home, he considered his assignment accomplished. Now, Tisa decided to call on headman Nkhanza to speak her mind.

'Baba, I have come here to tell you something that has been on my mind for the whole week,' she informed the headman. 'I want us to discuss the njazi problem. When my husband arrived, he told his brother that he did not want to talk to him. I do not like that. I want the two brothers to reconcile. I wish to ask you to convey my messages to both of them.'

'What should I tell them, mama?'

'Tell Baba Shuzi that I am sorry about the misunderstanding that occurred between us. I do not want it to happen again. Inform him that I will never again do anything that might offend him. Let him know that I wish to drink the nthumo with him.'

'Mama, those are words. I will convey the message to your brother-in-law. What should I tell your husband?'

'Please give him the same message. Tell him that I would like to drink the nthumo with my brother-in-law in order to put an end to this misunderstanding between the two families.'

'And if he refuses to talk to his brother?'

'I do not expect him to refuse for I will speak to him before you approach him.'

Headman Nkhanza briefed his nduna.

'I am ashamed of us,' the nduna said. 'Mother of Isaki is the one who thinks like a man. The men have not behaved like men.'

'Do not worry. Let us play our part. We must talk to Shuzi and Musandivute. Mother of Isaki awaits their responses.'

Whilst headman Nkhanza and his nduna talked to Shuzi, Tisa was talking to her husband. She did not want him to be taken by surprise when the two men approached him.

'Tisa, what is wrong with you?' asked Musa. 'You are not going to drink the nthumo with Shuzi. It is not your fault that we are not talking to each other. He brought about this misunderstanding between us. If we do not talk to each other, he is the one who will suffer.'

'You are wrong, baba. If this njazi stays in force, Baba Shuzi will not be the only one to suffer. You need your brother. Besides, he is your only brother. When I received your letter, I was sad that you were out there all on your own. I did not want you to die where there would be nobody to mourn you. I wanted you back here in your birthplace. I wanted you to be near your only brother.

'When Isaki brought you, I was relieved. I was happy for I knew that I had not waited in this village for seventeen years in vain. If you are going to live without talking to your brother, the purpose for which Isaki brought you home will be defeated. I would like us all to be happy. If we cannot drink the nthumo, it will be useless for me to continue living in this village. I will have to go to Mtendere until such time that you are in a position to agree to my drinking the nthumo,' said Tisa.

'And if Shuzi refuses to drink the nthumo?' asked Musa.

'I do not expect him to refuse. All he wanted was an apology from me and I have conveyed that through the headman.'

'Tisa, how can I thank you?'

'You do not have to. I am doing all this because I would like our marriage to come back to what it was before you were led astray by the devil. Can I read some scripture to you?'

'Yes, please.'

'Thank you,' she said as she rose to fetch her Bible.

She turned to the first Book of Corinthians chapter seven, verses ten and eleven which she read out aloud to him.

> *To the married I give this command (not I, but*
> *the Lord): A wife must not separate from her*

husband. But if she does, she must remain unmarried
or else be reconciled to her husband. And a husband
must not divorce his wife.

'Tisa, can I ask you something? What made you remain in this village for so long?'

'Faith.'

'Was that all?'

'That was all. I went by faith. And this has been my source of strength,' she added, lifting up her Bible. 'May I read you one more scripture?' she asked and proceeded to read from Mark chapter eleven, verses twenty-three and twenty-four:

I tell you the truth, if anyone says to this mountain,
'Go, throw yourself into the sea,' and does not doubt
in his heart but believes that what he says will happen,
it will be done for him. Therefore I tell you, whatever
you ask for in prayer, believe that you have received
it, and it will be yours.

'That is what made me persevere – the Word of God,' Tisa told her husband.

At that moment, headman Nkhanza and his nduna were approaching her compound. She stopped talking to her husband and waited for their arrival. She was anxious to hear whether her brother-in-law had accepted her apologies or not. She had been praying that he agreed to drink the nthumo with her. If he refused, she would be disappointed for she had already convinced her husband that it was in everyone's interest to end the njazi. Moreover, she had assured her husband that she did not expect his brother to turn down her apology.

'Obaba, do you bring good news or not?' she asked headman Nkhanza and his nduna as soon as they had sat down.

'Yes, mama,' the headman told her.

They had been successful with Shuzi. As Tisa discussed the matter with her husband, headman Nkhanza and his nduna conveyed her message to Shuzi.

'Baba Shuzi,' headman Nkhanza had begun, 'we are back here to discuss the issue of njazi between you and your sister-in-law. We have been sent by mother of Isaki to tell you that she is sorry about all the misunderstanding that has existed between you and her,' headman Nkhanza had continued. At this, Shuzi had sat up and decided to take the two emissaries seriously.

'She sends her sincere apologies to you and is asking you to drink the nthumo with her,' headman Nkhanza had gone on. 'What have you to say?'

'What can I say? This is what I always wanted from her. But now, is it not too late? If she had apologised before my brother returned, we would have gone ahead with the nthumo without any hindrance. But now my brother is so angry with me that he will not let us drink the nthumo even if both mother of Isaki and I agree to do so.'

'Your brother will not be a problem because mother of Isaki promised me that she was going to talk to him.'

'My sister-in-law promised that? That is wonderful. What has led to her change of heart? Please, convey my sincere gratitude to her. Tell her I look forward to drinking the nthumo with her.'

Both Tisa and her husband were happy to hear that Shuzi had agreed to drink the nthumo. And so were headman Nkhanza and the nduna.

'Now that you have all agreed to drink the nthumo, leave the rest to me,' said headman Nkhanza. 'I will have to find the best medicine man around.'

In spite of the great reconciliation that had taken place between his wife Tisa and himself on the one hand, and that between his wife and his brother on the other, Musa remained a worried and depressed man. That night, he did not get much sleep. He tossed about on the reed mat that had become his bed. Yes, Tisa was happy he was back in the village. His brother was happy and so was headman Nkhanza. They all had their reasons for celebrating his return. But he was not entirely without problems.

He was worried about Rhoda and his two daughters in Rhodesia. Would he ever see them again? And Rhoda? What would she think of him? He had not informed her that he had finally returned to his village. He wondered why she had not responded to the letter he sent her from Kitwe. He could go back to Rhodesia for her but she would not agree to leave her motherland. She had told him on many occasions that she did not want to come to Zambia with him because she had heard that there was a lot of witchcraft.

What made his heart burn with worry was the fact that she was still attractive enough to get married quickly. Perhaps some wealthy man had already married her. There was no way he would know that.

How he wished Rhoda could read those parts of the Bible which Tisa had been reading during the seventeen years he had been away! Those were good scriptures. Tisa had told him that she had spent seventeen years waiting for him to return because she had been guided by the Word of God. But no, Rhoda did not read the same parts of the Bible as Tisa read. Even if she did, she would not follow what they said as religiously as Tisa had done during the seventeen years that he had been away.

He thought of the household goods he had left in her father's custody. Would he ever get them back? There was no way he could replace them. He was going to lose them. Her father would sell them. Perhaps he had already sold them. Rhoda's father had probably made a fortune out of the sale of Musa's goods. He wished he could go back to Rhodesia for his property and for Rhoda and his daughters. But Tisa may not let him go. And it was her approval he needed.

GLOSSARY

baas: boss or master

baba: father; polite form of addressing any adult male (plural: obaba)

Cilapalapa: a pidgin containing features of Afrikaans, English and Bantu languages (see also Fanakalo)

citelele dance: a traditional dance among the Ngoni people of Zambia in which only women and girls participate

cimalo: marriage price

Fanakalo: a pidgin containing features of Afrikaans, English and Zulu (see also Cilapalapa)

kachasu: an illicit distilled alcoholic drink

kaphaso: a chief's body guard and messenger

kapitao: captain

malowolo: price paid by a man to his parents-in-law in addition to the marriage price in order to secure custody of children in case of a divorce

mama: mother; polite form of addressing any adult female (plural: omama)

misisi: from English missis/missus

muchona: a person who stays away from home for a long time; sojourner (plural: machona)

muti: medicinal charm

muzungu: a white man

nduna: deputy village headman

njazi: a curse believed to cause death through lightning

nsima: a thick maize meal porridge served with meat, fish or vegetables

nthumo: medicine used as an antidote to the curse of njazi; so called because it is drunk from gourd cup (nthumo)

pikinini: piccaninny

thobwa: a sweet non-alcoholic drink brewed from maize meal and millet

vipheko: beer brewed specially for a deserving son-in-law by his parents-in-law